Dreaming At the Top of My Lungs

Israel Finn

For Eyde

FOREWORD

What if? That's how it always starts—with that imperative tug inside the fiction writer's head, pulling him persistently out of what we call the real world and into that other one. The romance writer may well imagine a tale of unrequited love. The literary novelist might be stirred by the idea of an Oedipus-type of story with a different twist.

Me, I wonder what would happen in the moments after one of the wings is sheared away from the airplane I'm flying in, ripped from the fuselage like a crispy Thanksgiving turkey wing and flung out into space, the broken bird with the screaming people inside spinning toward the earth, and death.

Why? What might happen to cause such a thing? Well, one of the maintenance guys forgot to tighten a screw, or check a rivet, or whatever, because he was thinking about the argument he had with his wife that morning.

Again, why? Well, it seems she's been acting pretty weird lately, and he suspects her of screwing around on him. What he doesn't know—but what I do—is that his wife is not having an affair at all, but a quiet nervous breakdown because she keeps seeing her dead brother's ghost flitting around the house.

And so now we're all going to die.

I think about the elevator cable snapping, the car plunging thirty floors, and looking into the other bloodless, stricken faces while my mind gibbers all the way down. Because pink rain has begun falling from a gray sky, and it burns like acid. It's already eaten a hole in the roof and, as luck would have it, found its way to the cable pulley.

Consequently, they're going to be scraping us up with spatulas.

Train wrecks. Car crashes. Murder and general mayhem.

Why do I think about this stuff? Moreover, what would ever possess me to write about it?

Actually, I think the second question springs from the first. If you eliminate the ghost and the caustic rain from the aforementioned scenarios, what's left are real fears. My fears. I live with them every single day. Maybe you do too.

So I write, and that chases away the ghosts, so to speak. It keeps me sane. Mostly. And anyway, it's cheaper than therapy. Maybe I include an element of fantasy in my work because it helps me keep it together in a world with more than enough real problems to go around. It creates a counterbalance.

Because really, at the end of the day, when the screws start to come lose—and they always do, eventually—it's what goes on out there in that place we call the real world that scares the hell out of me.

STRANDED

I miss you. I think of you always. And if you never come back to me, I pray you're at least happy wherever you are right now.

It's always the dead of February. The tarnished sun sits frozen just above the rooftops in a low monochrome sky. I stand on the front porch of my house on Michigan Street and smoke a cigarette and watch for the girl. I don't have long to wait. A moment later she emerges from behind the house across the street and to my right, moving toward me along the cracked and canted walkway that runs beside the place. Somewhere a bird twitters. I scratch my beard and let my eyes crawl up her long blue jean-clad legs to the curves beneath her black suede jacket. I slide my tongue over my chapped lips. Finally I look into her impassive brown eyes. Their indifference mocks me. Choking back a sob, I look away, consumed by need and impotent rage, sick to my stomach with self-loathing.

I clamp the cigarette between my teeth and thrust my hands in the pockets of my sheepskin coat, drawing it tighter around me. It's one of those Midwest winter days when the air is so bitter it stings your cheeks and freezes the snot in your nose. Down the street on my left, a rust-eaten pickup truck crosses Michigan, going north on Monroe. It backfires, the blast rolling across the rooftops like a gunshot.

It typically takes the girl fifteen seconds to walk past the side of the two-story house with its chipped and faded pea green paint, at which point she rounds the building and heads west along the sidewalk. I watch from my side of the street as she passes the three neglected houses with their crumbling shingle roofs. As she walks past the last house on the corner—a shabby gray bungalow—her fingers lightly brush the low rusty chain-link fence guarding its dead brown patch of front yard. It takes the girl another fifteen seconds to reach the corner of Michigan and Garfield, where she turns on her heel and heads away from me and disappears from sight on the other side of the bungalow—to instantly, impossibly reappear at the back of the faded green house again, walking toward me exactly as before. No half a minute on the flipside. No in between. No nothing. The bird chirps. The pickup passes.

When it started I remember calling out to the girl after her fourth or fifth trip around the house across the street, "Hey, do you have a twin, or what?"

She turned up her nose and stormed off, and I realized she must have mistaken my question for impropriety. But when she came round again she seemed completely unruffled.

Then all at once I knew. My body jerked as if from an electric shock. I backpedaled and slammed against the storm door, crying out. I began to babble. In a fantasy story, that was the moment when the hero would have thought he had gone insane. But I was no hero and this was no story. I knew that what was happening was real. Still my mind railed against it, thrashing like a wild animal caught in a trap. I drew a shuddering breath, then let loose a terrible scream. The girl cast a startled glance over her shoulder, her eyes briefly meeting mine, before hurrying around the corner again. In the blink of an eye, she reappeared at the back of the green house and came walking toward me once more, her face perfectly serene—that is, until she noticed the howling lunatic across the street. Because that's how it is. Her motions and expressions are as unchanging as that perpetual sun. Unless I intervene. For a while I did, but not so much anymore.

I call her Alicia. That's because she never tells me her real name, though I've asked her more times than I can count. Besides, she looks like an Alicia, and I need to call her something. Hers is the only face I've seen in a long, long time. It's impossible to say just how long. Maybe a year. Maybe more. Things never change here, so there's really no way to tell. It doesn't matter, because I've found out the hard way that marking the time isn't nearly as important as passing it. I do what I can with what I have, which isn't much. Occasionally I just sit and think, though more and more often that seems to be a dangerous course, because when the monotony closes over you like a shroud you can find your thoughts turning to things best left unconsidered. And lately I've come to believe that my mind has a mind of its own, and I fear my thoughts are out to get me. Whenever the voices in my head start getting too loud I reach for *David Copperfield*, and each time I do I'm struck by the memory, the irony, that I couldn't have cared less when you first tossed the book on the coffee table.

I'm screaming again, the hot steam of my breath torn apart on the frigid air. It's always the same. Alicia stops and stares at me with wide, frightened eyes. Between screams the bird twitters. From a window in the house across the way a shadowy figure watches me from the dimness beyond the glass. As I shriek I see the pickup truck go past from the corner of my eye. It backfires. The dark shape at the window dissolves. Then Alicia vanishes into thin air, only to reappear a heartbeat later at the back corner of the green house again, sauntering toward me with that Mona Lisa smile on her face, completely oblivious that we are locked in hell together.

I'm allowed no more than thirty seconds—less, if I try to step beyond my house—before I rematerialize on the front porch again. But I remain in possession of any object I'm able to get a hold of within that time frame, so long as I remain awake. I grab cold cuts and crackers, potables, fruits and nuts from my perpetually stocked kitchen. I take a quick whore's bath at the sink in the tiny downstairs half bath (sans razors) and use its toilet if I have the time, which I usually don't. If not, I go wherever is convenient, unconcerned about the mess. It disappears half a minute later. My clothes remain unsoiled—I assume because they're not a part of my body—but my hair and beard are a lost cause. Alicia must think I'm a fright. Mostly I stay put on the porch since it's where I end up every thirty seconds in any case. I tug my sheepskin coat securely around me, and I hear my mother's voice warning me once again that I'm going to catch my death. Then I lose myself in Dickens while smoking cigarettes from the inexhaustible pack on my coffee table. Sometimes I hunker out of sight with my back against the porch's low brick wall and do needful, shameful things to myself. Other times I curl up in a ball and weep until my eyes are red and swollen. Then exhaustion claims me, and I fall asleep on the cold hard concrete and dream of you.

I can't get to the upstairs office in time. I can just make it to the doorway. Beyond that, our books stand sentinel on their shelves and my cellphone lies next to the computer keyboard where I left it when I took a break from writing to come down and have a smoke. Reaching the books would be a triumph in itself, but it's the phone I want. Yet I barely make the threshold, my gaze falling through the doorway upon a dead world that, for all intents and purposes, might as well be a thousand light years away. Then I'm snatched back to the porch. Not that reaching the phone would change anything, but I'd sell my soul to hear your voice again, if only for a moment. And tell you I'm sorry.

What I wouldn't give to take it all back—the awful things I said to you. When you came home from running errands I was in one of my funks. I stood at the storm door with a cigarette in my mouth and my silver Zippo in my hand, preparing to step out onto the porch and observe my smoker's ritual. That's when you made a detour on your way to the kitchen, saying, "Gotcha this." I heard something thump onto the coffee table and gave it a grudging glance. It was *David Copperfield.* I grunted noncommittally as you breezed into the kitchen and began unpacking a sack of groceries. You were in high spirits, going on and on about your afternoon.

It didn't take me long to kill that.

It wasn't your fault that my first novel was dead in the water, or that I had to be at my dreary office job early the next morning. You weren't to blame for my feeling ordinary and overlooked. But I managed to take it out on you anyway, because it was easier than looking in the mirror.

I never blamed you directly, but I never had to, did I? My self-imposed anguish was always there, hanging over me like a black cloud, and you could never get too close to me without stepping into its shadow.

I met your chatter with a wall of stony silence. Finally you stopped in mid-sentence, poked your head into the living room and asked if I was okay.

"I'm fine."

I could feel you on tenterhooks, watching me.

I remained silent. Closed off. Just stood there at the door looking resentfully out at a world that was passing me by.

You entered the room hesitantly, as if you were venturing into a cave with an ill-tempered, bee-stung bear. "Honey, what's the matter?" you probed.

"Nothing."

"It's not 'nothing.' Do you want to talk about it?"

"No."

"It might help to get it off your chest."

"I told you I don't want to talk about it."

Then you said, "Is it your book?"

I remember thinking, Okay, you asked for it, and suddenly I was lashing out, launching into one of my famous tirades. I said it wasn't just my lousy book, it was our lousy *life*, our dull *excuse* for a life. Told you I was sick to death of the grueling, mind-numbing repetition. Every day was the same as the next, and I'd had it, absolutely had it. I was done. I'm not altogether sure what I meant by that last part. I was in a red fog. All I know is that you tried to reach out to me, tried to talk me down like you always did when I got that way. But I was determined to wallow in my own misery, and I pigheadedly turned you aside. I'll never forget the hurt look on your face when I said I wished you would just go away and leave me alone. You said, "Okay, if that's what you want," and you walked out the door with your keys in your hand.

And I'll never forget what I shouted after you: "What I want is just *thirty goddamn seconds a day to myself!"*

It's always the dead of February. The tarnished sun sits frozen just above the rooftops in a low monochrome sky. I stand on the front porch of my house on Michigan Street and smoke a cigarette and watch for the girl. I don't have long to wait.

NO SUCH THING AS MONSTERS

Dickey woke with a start when his bedroom door banged open. He jerked his head up and saw a hulking figure slumping in the doorway, and his first groping thought was that the thing that lived under his bed had finally gotten free and was now loose in the house. It shambled forward, letting in the dull lamplight from the living room at the end of the hallway. Shadows danced and capered on the walls, then fell still as the thing stood looming over him. Dickey sensed its cold eyes measuring him in the half-light, smelled its stinking hot breath—actually felt it blasting against his face—and almost let loose in his Spiderman underwear.

Then the thing rolled its head languidly on its thick neck and, when it was angled toward the lambent light just so, Dickey recognized his father's face. His relief at being delivered from the thing that bedeviled his dreams was at first so intense that he forgot to be afraid of the one who made his waking life hell. That is, until his dad said, "You little fuck."

Then Dickey remembered.

The stink on his father's breath came from the bottle of Wild Turkey on the kitchen counter. Dickey associated that smell with fear. Hopelessness. And pain. Sober, his dad was at best quiet and moody, and a careless remark was liable to earn you the back of his hand. Drunk, he could be downright dangerous. When he was like that it was best to be someplace else if you didn't want to wind up in the emergency room at the county hospital. Both Dickey and his mom could vouch for that. His dad called those times "bad spells."

Dickey had an idea the bad spells had something to do with the place his dad had gone away to for a while when Dickey was just a kid. He vaguely remembered visiting once or twice with his mom, but it was mostly fuzzy in his head: gray-green walls and windows with wire in them. Men in white coats. The smell of Lysol. After his dad came back home, Dickey overheard quiet phone conversations between his mom and his aunt, whom Dickey barely knew and who lived way out in California.

"He's feelin' much better now, Nora," his mom would say, and, "I think the pills are workin'. He don't lose his temper like before. I mean, sure, he still gets a little riled up now and then, but it ain't nearly as bad as it was. I think it's finally gonna be okay."

But she was wrong. And Dickey discovered that there were worse things in the world than imaginary monsters under the bed. He knew there was really no such thing, anyway. Didn't need to be. There were plenty of real monsters on the loose.

"I saw you runnin' through my tomato patch today," his dad said now. "Just runnin' and playin' like you didn't have a care in the whole goddamn world. And knockin' my stakes every which way with no nevermind at all."

A slight movement caused Dickey to drop his eyes and he saw that his dad held a rusty saw—the one from the woodshed—in his right hand. The movement that had drawn Dickey's gaze was the flexing of the man's hand on the grimy wooden grip. Squeezing and relaxing, over and over, like a beating heart.

His father leaned in and flung Dickey's Batman sheet aside in one quick motion, then seized Dickey's right leg in a vice-like grip. Dickey yelped and began chanting, *"Bad spell bad spell bad spell Daddy bad spell . . ."*

The big man set the sharp teeth of the saw blade against his son's tender leg, just below the knee. Dickey looked down in shock and saw a bead of blood drip down his inner calf. He had visions of his future self, confined to a wheelchair.

Dickey's mom was working the night shift at the diner in town, and their nearest neighbors, the Hillmans, lived over a mile away on the other side of the big woods. Screaming would do him no good.

Dickey screamed.

"Well," said his dad with a good-humored grin, "you ain't never gonna do that again, you little cocksucker. I guaran-goddamn-*tee* it!"

"Please, Daddy, no," Dickey begged, his hands fluttering uselessly at his father's brawny arms like two tiny white birds. "No no *pleeeeeease!*" And then his bladder actually did let go.

"This is gonna hurt you more than it will me," Dickey's dad said, then giggled. He began to draw back the blade.

In that moment there was a loud crunch of bone, but Dickey felt no pain. His dad's mouth formed an O and he suddenly sprang upright, dropping the saw flat across Dickey's legs. He was flung backward as if a rug had been yanked out from under his feet, though no rug was there. He crashed down with the force of a felled tree, his head thumping the hardwood floor like a melon, and the sudden impact shook the house to its core. A flowerpot Dickey had made in art class danced to the edge of his dresser, jumped off and shattered.

Dickey's dad began to shriek. His body was being dragged beneath the bed by something, and when the man looked to see what it was, his face crumpled and he started to sob. He was hauled unceremoniously out of sight. Dickey heard the eager rending of flesh and bone, felt something heavy bucking against the underside of his bed. Then the sound of his father's wailing was suddenly cut off. For what seemed like forever there was only dead silence. Dickey lay still as a stone in the middle of it.

Then he heard a long, satisfied belch, followed by the sound of a dark chuckle under there.

OVER MY DEAD BODY

Eddie Merrick couldn't shake the feeling. Like something was about to happen. Something bad. The sensation was so strong, so *intense,* it felt like a presence occupied actual space on the seat beside him.

He wondered if maybe he shouldn't have heisted the car on a Friday night. And on Halloween. Way too many people out and about. But he hadn't been able to resist the shiny new 1940 Ford Coupe sitting in the parking lot of Murphy's Bar with the keys dangling in the ignition like an invitation. He swore this was the last time. One more good score and he'd get out of this town, go somewhere with a lot of trees. Get an honest job. Now, sitting behind the wheel of the car, he couldn't wait to get rid of it. He estimated pulling into Paulie's Garage in fifteen minutes, give or take. Another ten minutes and he'd be handing the keys to this bucket over to Paulie himself. As he hung a left onto Jersey Avenue Eddie felt a crawling sensation in his testicles and along his spine. Like someone was watching him.

You're just antsy. You think because it's your last time, you're gonna get pinched. Stop being so superstitious.

He switched on the car radio and got the news. A man's nasally, urgent voice said that the president promised not to send "our boys" into the war. Eddie didn't believe it. If Roosevelt planned on keeping the U.S. out of it, then why had he enacted the draft? The Jerrys wouldn't be happy until they took over the whole damn world. Eddie had seen Hitler a few times on the newsreels. A man that relentless wouldn't stop until you *stopped* him. Looking for a way out of his dead-end life, Eddie had tried to join the Army four years ago, on his eighteenth birthday. They turned him down flat because of his bum leg. When he was thirteen, Eddie's old man beat him unconscious with a baseball bat for bringing home a bad report card. Eddie had never hated the drunken bastard more than he did the day he left the recruiter's office with that rejection slip in his hand.

Eddie soon tired of the news. He fiddled with the radio until he came across a station playing his favorite song, Glenn Miller's "In The Mood." He took it as a good omen and hummed along with the tune. He turned right onto Mercer Street and gunned the engine. There was a flash of bright red through the windshield. He mashed his foot down on the brake pedal—a second too late. There was a sickening thump as the car collided with whatever had crossed its path. The Ford screeched to a halt, and Eddie stared out past the gleaming black hood, his fingers wrapped around the steering wheel in a death grip, cold sweat prickling his skin. Someone screamed and Eddie's head snapped around. At the curb stood a girl and a boy, dressed respectively as a witch and a pirate. From the witch's right hand dangled a plastic jack-o'-lantern bucket. In her left hand, she gripped a broom. The pirate carried his booty in a white paper bag with a picture of a skull and crossbones on the side. A black eyepatch covered one eye while the other eye gazed in shock at the red clump in the middle of the street.

The radio was still blasting "In The Mood." Eddie reached out with trembling fingers and switched it off. The sudden silence was deafening. He got out of the car and, his heart thudding in his chest, limped toward the red bundle.

It was a little girl. Dressed like Red Riding Hood. She lay on her back a good thirty feet beyond the car's grill, awash in the headlamps like an actress playing a death scene on a stage. And dead she was; if the enormous amount of blood pooling around her head didn't tell you the story, her open and vacant eyes sure as hell did. She had landed in such a way that the back of her skull had cracked open like a raw egg. An insane and unbidden thought arose in Eddie's mind: *You gotta break a few eggs to make an omelet.* He felt his gorge rise.

"Margaret?" said the witch in a tiny voice. She was twelve or thirteen. "Get up, Margaret."

The boy, who was much younger, rolled an accusing blue eye toward Eddie. "You ran over our sister. You're a bad man." Then a single tear welled up in that eye and spilled down his cheek.

Eddie thought this couldn't be happening. But he looked down at the dead girl's face, at the empty eyes staring up into the night sky, and knew it was. Panic wrapped its icy fingers around him. Without thinking, he made the sign of the cross, a buried ritual from his childhood.

Margaret had been toting a jack-o'-lantern bucket, like her big sister. It had rolled away against the far curb like a severed head, spilling its contents all over the street the same way Margaret's head had spilled its own.

The witch screamed again. Eddie looked up. Other trick-or-treaters had gathered. Faces were appearing at windows in some of the nearby houses. The commotion had drawn a few people out onto their porches. For one insane moment, it occurred to Eddie to explain to the onlookers what had happened here. *She came out of nowhere, folks, I swear. I was just minding my business, out for a little spin on a Friday night and listening to Glenn Miller on the radio when she stepped right out in front of me. And I haven't had a drop to drink, either. Sober as the Pope on Sunday morning. Oh, the car? Well, it's like this....*

Two guys hurried across their lawns toward the street. The witch-girl was still screaming, a terrible piercing cry that set Eddie's teeth on edge and blended with another, similar sound: the distant approach of police sirens.

Eddie took off. Didn't know in what direction, and didn't care. As long as it was *away*. He hopped fences and shambled across backyards, leaving in his wake barking dogs, trampled flowers, and dented garbage cans. He lurched through side streets, between houses, and down dark alleys. Hid behind trees or parked cars whenever he saw headlamps coming toward him. When he entered an alley at one point Eddie observed a flow of people streaming past at the other end of it. He decided getting lost in a crowd would be his best bet for escape. Slowing his pace, Eddie attempted to pull himself together as he approached the alley's exit. He entered the street and shuffled along the sidewalk, trying to blend in with the crowd.

He was on Newark Avenue. First chance he got he'd grab a cab and take it across the river into New York. Then he'd lay low for a while until he could figure something out. He didn't hold out much hope though; his prints were all over the Coupe. And a couple of those folks would be able to pick him out of a lineup, no sweat.

There were a lot of costumed people on the street, adult partygoers celebrating the holiday and the weekend ahead. He passed Frankenstein's monster and his bride, and as he eyeballed them, Eddie bumped into Superman.

"Watch it, Mac," the man of steel warned, and then stuck a fat cigar in his pie hole.

Eddie saw a cowboy with his arm around an Indian squaw, and a spaceman wearing a silver suit and what looked like a large fishbowl over his head. The whole atmosphere lent a sense of unreality to an already bizarre situation.

The marquee of the Palace Theater loomed up ahead. As Eddie drew near he became confused. He had passed the Palace only an hour ago, on his way (unbeknownst to him at the time) to steal the Ford. The theater had been showing the new movie by Charlie Chaplain, *The Great Dictator*. Eddie remembered because he had made a note he wanted to see it over the weekend. Now the marquee read *The Conjuring 2*. Eddie frowned. He had never heard of *The Conjuring* 1, much less its sequel. Had the Chaplain movie been damaged?

These thoughts were purely sensory, fleeting, there one minute and gone the next. Deeper down, Eddie's mind shouted out the absolute certainty that the cops were hunting for him at that exact moment. And the real possibility that they were closing in on him.

A city bus lumbered by on its way to the bus stop half a block down the street. On its side was an advertisement. Eddie had seen nothing like it before, and he gaped at it. It was showy, splashed with bright purples and yellows that made his head hurt. The ad featured two palookas grinning like monkeys. Screaming in bright red letters a foot and a half tall was the message MORNING DRIVE-TIME WITH PHIL AND THE ROOSTER! And under that, only a fraction less gaudy: 105.1 The Kick—Jersey City's #1 Rock-and-roll radio!

Eddie didn't know what to think, except *What the hell is rock-and-roll?* As he approached its stop, Eddie watched the bus pull to the curb and spill its passengers onto the sidewalk. They all went their separate ways, and there was nothing remarkable about any of them, but one. She moved along the sidewalk in his direction, lighting a cigarette as she came. Tattered denim shorts barely covered her midsection and ripped black stockings ran down her long legs to a pair of scuffed army boots. The arms of a flannel shirt were cinched around her waist. She wore a black t-shirt, the name RAMONES emblazoned in white across her jiggling breasts. Her blonde hair was longish on one side, buzzed to a bristle on the other, and her face and ears flashed with so many metal rings and thingamabobs she looked like a human pincushion. Eddie found himself appalled and aroused at the same time.

As she passed, the girl sneered at him. "Fuck you lookin' at?" she demanded. Eddie turned to watch her stalk away, and she shot over her shoulder, "Take a goddamn picture, why don'tcha? Asshole."

Eddie looked around. No one else was paying the slightest attention to the spectacle. He didn't understand. How could people not notice her? What the hell was going on? He realized his mouth was hanging open and snapped it shut.

Then it occurred to him that the girl's outlandish getup must have been a Halloween costume. She was headed to a party. Sure, that had to be it. Still, he'd seen nothing like her before. Also, Eddie had never heard a woman talk like that, and he'd spent time with some pretty crazy dames. Bewildered, he turned and continued on his way.

And damned if he didn't feel eyes on him again. He tried to ignore it; if he lost his head, he'd never get out of this in one piece.

As he passed the bus stop, he noticed a newsboy hawking his wares there in the middle of the busy sidewalk. The kid clasped a few papers in one hand while waving a single copy in the air with the other.

"Extra! Extra! Read all about it!" the boy announced to anyone who would listen. "Italian troops invade Greece! Greeks launch strong counter-offensive!"

Eddie scanned the street for a cab. No luck.

The newsie shouted. "Forty-seven German aircraft shot down above England!"

A guy in a gray suit stopped for a paper. He flipped the boy a nickel, and there was a brief flash of silver before the kid snatched it out of the air.

Nothing Eddie could do. He'd just have to hoof it for now. At least every step he took was taking him farther away from Mercer Street, and the dead girl.

Margaret, his mind spoke up. *If you're gonna run a little girl down, you should have the decency to remember her name.*

Yeah, well, he argued, it's not like I meant to do it. So why turn myself in now? Me going to the big house isn't gonna bring her back.

He remembered the little pirate calling him a bad man. But he wasn't. Sure, he was no saint. He'd pulled a few jobs in his time. But he never bumped anybody off.

Until now.

I didn't do it on *purpose,* goddamn it, he countered.

The newsboy yelled, "Airliners bring down twin towers in New York City in terrorist attack!"

Eddie halted and cast a side-long glance at the kid. What the hell was he talking about? Had the Krauts attacked the city? What twin towers?

Then the boy cried, "Petty thief, Eddie Merrick, wanted for the hit-and-run murder of Margaret May Dowling!"

Eddie felt his heart lurch painfully in his chest. Now the newsie looked straight at him. Holding the stack of newspapers straight out in front of him like a billboard, the kid flashed a sinister grin and tipped Eddie a wink. Eddie couldn't breathe. He was pictured on the front page next to the girl. Eddie's picture was a mug shot from two years ago, a bit he did for a burglary rap. Margaret's image was from tonight. It showed her splayed out on the street, broken and bloody, her eyes staring at nothing. The angle of the shot was from Eddie's perspective as he had stood looking down at her. As if he'd taken the picture.

A moan rose from deep in his throat as Eddie backed away from the newsboy. He stumbled at the curb and nearly toppled into the path of an oncoming car. Regained his balance at the last second, but overcompensated, and pitched forward onto his hands and knees. But he was up again in an instant, reeling down the street, thinking that this was it, this was what it felt like to flip your wig. But another part of him—the Eddie Fucking Merrick part—fought to silence his gibbering mind. There's a reasonable explanation. I'm just paranoid, that's all. I'm tense and my mind's playing tricks on me.

But he needed to get the hell out of this town right now. He searched the street again for a cab, but several outlandish-looking cars in the midst of the regular traffic drove him to distraction.

What is this?

He didn't have too long to dwell on the question, though, because from the corner of his eye, Eddie swore he saw someone in a red hood and cape across the street a little farther down. Just as he focused on them, however, they disappeared down an alley. Eddie limp-skipped along his side of the street until he drew even with the alley's entrance, and saw it was not an alley at all, just a brick wall set back between two buildings. There was nowhere the owner of the red hood could have disappeared *to*.

You're off your rocker.

Shut up, he told himself.

He craned his neck looking for a cab but saw none. Where the hell were they? They should be out in droves tonight. There must be a million Halloween bashes. He cursed under his breath and turned to go—and ran smack into Snow White carrying an assortment of liquor bottles in a paper bag. The bag tipped and threatened to dump its contents, and she and Eddie did an awkward dance together there on the sidewalk under the streetlights, trying to prevent disaster. After a moment during which things might have gone either way, fortune won out.

"Well, excuse you," she said and snickered.

"I'm awfully sorry," Eddie said. "I'm in a hurry and wasn't—"

"Aw"—she waved it away—"don't give it a second thought."

Eddie offered her a polite smile.

The girl gave him the once-over. "Say, fella. Are you okay? You don't look so hot."

"I'm swell," Eddie said. "Listen, I gotta—"

"You're white as a sheet. Look like you seen a ghost, or somethin'"

Eddie gaped at her.

"Oh my goodness!" she exclaimed, and Eddie jumped. "I can't believe I said that—that you look like you seen a ghost. On Halloween!" She brayed with laughter.

Eddie gave an embarrassed glance around at the passersby.

Snow White thrust out her free hand. "I'm Edna."

He shook with her. "E-Eddie."

"Hey! Eddie and Edna!"

She was a dish. Just not too bright. Or maybe she'd already been hitting the hooch.

"Well, it's nice t' meet you, Eddie. I think we—"

She stopped dead. She stood there, frozen.

"Um… Edna?" Eddie mumbled.

Edna's frozen smile became a rictus. Her brow wrinkled in confusion, and her eyes rolled away from his as she observed her surroundings as if for the first time. The bag slipped from her grasp and the booze smashed on the concrete, after all, filling the air with the sharp smell of whiskey. Edna's face transformed into a mask of abject misery. Her eyes were filled with tears when they fell on Eddie's face again. The tears spilled down her cheeks as she stared at him with a horrifying, mournful expression. And in a voice that made Eddie's blood run cold, she said, "Where am I?" She reached out and seized Eddie's arms in a claw-like grip. "What is this place?"

Eddie cried out and tore himself away. He fled, leaving her standing there in the middle of the sidewalk.

She screamed after him, "WHERE AM I?"

He said a prayer under his breath, one of many they had taught him to recite as a kid, between beatings from his old man. He could only remember the first part, so he kept repeating it over and over. "Hail Mary, full of grace. The Lord is with thee. Hail Mary, full of grace. The Lord is with thee. Hail Mary, full of grace. The Lord is with thee..."

He had gone a block when he stopped in his tracks, his heart hammering in his chest. Heading toward him was a clown, a guy dressed as Dracula, a hula dancer in a grass skirt and a coconut bra. And a cop. They were all laughing and shooting the breeze and hadn't yet noticed Eddie. Eddie didn't know if the copper's uniform was a Halloween costume or the real deal. But he wasn't taking any chances. Beads of sweat popping up on his brow, he looked around for a place to duck into and spotted a bar across the street, with the name Angelo's above the door.

Eddie crossed Newark Avenue against the flow of traffic, which had become a little backed up. Upon closer inspection, he decided that some of the odd-looking automobiles were in fact quite sleek, if a little unimaginative. As he crossed, there came from somewhere among the vehicles, music the likes of which Eddie had never heard or even imagined. You couldn't even call it music, he thought. What were those hellish instruments? And the "singer" was screaming like he was in pain. Eddie continued across the street, relieved to reach the other side. With a casual glance over his shoulder to make sure he wasn't being hounded by the cop, Eddie slipped into Angelo's.

The first thing to catch his eye in the low light was the glowing television. At least, that's what he assumed it must be. He didn't own one himself, never saw much use in them, though he had seen them around, even nabbed one in a burglary once. But he had never seen a television anywhere like this one. Something inside him cried out in denial because he knew it didn't belong here. Mounted near the ceiling in one corner behind the bar, its huge picture tube (must have been four feet wide!) was alive with color and motion. A football game was on, the picture so vivid that Eddie half expected a player to run out of the box and into the room.

There was a guy at one of the tables who had his own personal television, a slim, flat thing that looked like it was part typewriter. He sat hunched over it, watching what looked to Eddie like a politician giving a speech. And then, to Eddie's surprise, the guy closed the thing up like a briefcase.

But the sight that bowled him over was the handheld gadgets that a couple of people seemed to use as both tiny televisions and some kind of walkie-talkies.

This is all wrong, Eddie thought. And it's been wrong since that spooky kid with the newspapers. Maybe even before that. Maybe…

You know when everything went wrong.

Yeah, he admitted. When I hit the girl. When I hit Margaret.

Think again.

At first, Eddie didn't understand. And it pissed him off. Then, he got it. And the answer was so simple.

He sighed. When I ran, Eddie told himself. It all came to pieces when I ran.

Give that man a cigar!

But what Eddie wanted was a belt.

He approached the bar, behind which worked a heavyset man with slicked-back black hair that was going gray around the temples. The guy wore an orange t-shirt with black letters that said WHY CAN'T WITCHES GET PREGNANT? THEIR HUSBANDS HAVE HOLLOW-WEENIES!

"Who's winning?" Eddie nodded at the television.

"This is a recording. Giants beat the Rams, thirty-one to ten." He shook his head. "L.A. sucks this season."

In as steady a voice as he was able, Eddie said, "I thought the Rams played in Cleveland."

The barkeep looked at Eddie in thoughtful consideration. Then he roared laughter. Two geezers at the other end of the bar glanced their way and then returned to their beer and conversation.

"Maybe they should," the barkeep said.

Eddie showed him a wooden smile.

"What'll it be?"

"Scotch, neat."

"Five bucks."

With trembling fingers, Eddie fished a fin out of his wallet and slid it across the bar.

The guy set him up and then strolled down the bar to chat with the two geezers. Eddie picked up his drink, swirled it around twice, anticipating the taste, then tossed it back.

Except the liquor didn't touch his lips. As Eddie looked on, the scotch drained from the glass backward. It receded into the upturned bottom and disappeared. It was as if the glass itself had drunk it.

His hand shaking badly now, Eddie set the glass back down on the bar—and watched it fill from nowhere to its original level again. He shook his head vigorously and lifted the glass again. He raised it to his lips.

The same thing happened as before; the scotch emptied into the glass.

With a frustrated cry, Eddie hurled the glass at the wall behind the bar where it exploded with the sound of a gunshot.

The barkeep yelled, "Hey, what the hell!" He dug one of those handheld gadgets out of his front pocket.

Eddie wasn't paying attention; he stared up at the television, where the picture had changed. On the screen, a Ford Coupe—his Ford Coupe—turned onto Mercer Street. Eddie could just hear Glenn Miller's "In The Mood" drifting through the open driver's side window. The camera pulled back, offering a wide view, just as a tiny figure in a red hood and cape stepped off the curb and into the street. The car struck the child's body like a giant steel fist, sending it flying through the air like a rag doll and—

Eddie turned his back. He'd seen enough. More than enough.

The patrons at the tables were all watching him.

The bartender poked Eddie hard between the shoulder blades. "Hey, you! Get the fuck out of here now! I called the cops."

Eddie didn't need to hear it twice. He stumbled to the door.

Outside, Margaret Dowling lay in the gutter.

Eddie's body stiffened in fear so suddenly that his spine popped.

She raised her head, and a ropy length of half-coagulated blood stretched between her crushed skull and the ground. She grinned, and Eddie saw that half her teeth were broken.

"How did it feel?" she asked him. It didn't sound like a little girl's voice. It sounded old.

A croaking noise rose from Eddie's throat.

"How did it feel to kill me?" A bit of brain dropped from the hole in her head and plopped onto the curb.

No, Eddie thought. Her voice doesn't just sound old. It sounds ancient. Wherever she went after dying, she was there for ages.

"How did it feel to stand there? To stand over my dead body and look down at it?"

Eddie tried to reply, tried to say he was sorry, that he'd take it back if he could. But he could only shake his head and stammer.

"HOW DID IT FEEL?" screamed the thing in the gutter.

Eddie bolted. Behind him, the ghost let loose a hideous wail, one that would have turned the bravest man into a coward, and it turned Eddie's guts to water. He barely noticed the piss running down his leg as he limp-skipped down the sidewalk, shoving people out of his way. His terror was mindless, and he may have gone on that way forever, or until his leg gave out or his heart burst. But then he saw the priest.

The old man was standing on the corner, waiting to cross the street, the shock of hair on his head as white as his collar. When he saw Eddie coming, his burning blue eyes seemed to get even more intense, as if a flame flared up behind them. A smile played on his lips.

Eddie skidded to a halt in front of the priest, clasping his hands together in supplication. But he dare not quite touch the man, because though Eddie had forsaken religion, years spent having it crammed down his throat had instilled in him a grudging respect for it, and in his heart, he felt unworthy. Unclean. "Please, father," he begged. "Help me."

"Help you with what, Eddie?"

"I didn't mean to hurt her, father I swear, I mean, I know I did wrong and all, heisting that Coupe, but I never… I never…"

Eddie trailed off. He looked at the priest. Then he said, "How do you know my name?"

The priest smiled, and Eddie saw the devil it. He still felt petrified of the thing that had once been Margaret Dowling, and yet it was dawning on him that he could run, but he couldn't hide.

"Oh, I know all about you, Eddie."

Eddie deflated. "So you're part of…" he shook his head and shrugged, "this… whatever's happening?"

"Indeed." The old man's blue eyes twinkled with that inner light.

Cars whooshed by on the street. On the sidewalk, people flowed past Eddie and the priest like they were two islands in a stream. Eddie barely noticed.

"Am I in hell?"

The priest gave no answer, but there was a knowing gleam in his eyes.

Eddie sighed. "Are you even a real priest?"

"Ha! God, no." He struck a pose. "This is my Halloween costume, worn especially for the occasion. Not bad, eh?"

Eddie just looked at him.

"Truth be told," the old man said, "I wear it to draw you to me. Despite your occupation, your Catholic upbringing still has a lot of power over you, Eddie. I could approach you, but it's not as…sporting."

"What the hell are you talking about?" Eddie shouted.

The old man smiled, unruffled. "James and Katherine Dowling were the parents of young Margaret. They were quite well off. Filthy rich, you might say.

"On the night you killed Margaret, the police came close to capturing you. A couple of the residents of Mercer Street got a good look at you and described you. You weren't hard to track down. They spotted you here on Newark Avenue, and they gave chase. It would have been better for you had they caught you, Eddie. As it was, you ran into the street—and smack in front of a moving bus. It killed you instantly."

"You're crazy," Eddie whispered.

The old man smiled. "Am I?"

Eddie said nothing.

"As I said, the Dowlings were wealthy. I won't bore you with the details, but suffice it to say that, over the years, James invested in several companies, leveraging his assets into a powerful empire. Where I'm from, Eddie, the Dowling family are giants.

"One company engaged in DNA research. I know you don't understand what I mean—not being a scientist, I don't understand it all, myself—but I'll explain things as best I can."

"I don't want to hear any more of this," Eddie said.

"Oh, Eddie," said the old man, "don't you know, you have no choice?"

Eddie fell silent. A passing car honked its horn, and he cringed.

"Now, where was I? Oh, yes. DNA—deoxyribonucleic acid. The carrier of genetic information and the building blocks of life.

"Again, it would have been better for you had the police captured you that night. You'd have done time, and that probably would have been the end of it. But you escaped punishment when you stepped in front of that bus. Some thought it was poetic justice since you died in the same manner as Margaret. But James and Katherine Dowling disagreed. As did I.

"Which is why we exhumed your bones and regenerated your body. And then placed that body in a suspended state. Oh, it looks nothing like the old you, I'm afraid. Just a gelatinous blob with a brain, floating in a biotic soup. Much of your nourishment comes from your own waste, which you release into the tank and recycle through your body.

"A computer is connected to your brain. It's used to control your memories and to create this place you see around you. I'm also able to visit you here personally from time to time, though we have to make certain adjustments for that. The program default runs much too fast for me to be here in real time, so you usually just encounter a smart projection of me. The thing is, the computer became self-aware of late and has rewritten the program on its own. That's why you're experiencing glimpses of a future you don't understand. And other anomalies, such as the young woman named Edna. She's nothing more than a glitch manifested by that self-awareness. At first, we planned to intervene, but I rather enjoy the surprises it springs on you. It keeps things interesting. Yes, I think we'll give the computer the benefit of the doubt for the foreseeable future.

"To answer your question, Eddie: no, you are not in hell. You're in prison."

So there it was.

"You're saying none of this"—Eddie gestured at everything around them—"is real?"

"It's as real as the pain you feel, Eddie. They say 'All the world's a stage.' Perhaps it should be 'All the worlds are stages.'"

Eddie now realized who he was talking to.

"You're the boy, aren't you? The pirate. Margaret's brother."

"Superb, Eddie! I'm Peter Dowling." That smile again. Those twinkling eyes.

Eddie felt numb.

"You'll never—*ever*—be allowed to experience pleasures of any kind here."

Eddie said, "The scotch."

"Yes. From here on out, there's only fear and frustration for you, my friend."

"And how long will that be?"

Dowling shrugged. "Forever."

"You've got to die sometime," Eddie reminded him.

"True." The old man nodded. "But my son is part of the operation right now. And someday my grandsons will take over. Besides, time means nothing here, Eddie. We can make a second seem like ages to you. You've already lived through this night millions of times."

"Please…" Eddie said.

"If there's a heaven I suppose your soul is in God's hands. But your ass—such as it is—belongs to us."

Eddie hung his head and cried.

"See you soon, Eddie," said Peter Dowling. "Oh. And happy Halloween."

Everything faded to black.

***

Eddie Merrick couldn't shake the feeling.

Like something was about to happen.

Something bad.

SICK DAY

Harold Weems staggered from his couch to his bathroom, coughing so forcibly that motes swam before his red, rheumy eyes. He felt awful—the worst bout of the flu he'd had since . . . well, ever. One minute shivering uncontrollably under his quilt, the next soaking it with sweat. At the moment, fever gripped him and heat radiated off him in waves. Delirium was closing in.

Still hacking, he lurched through the bathroom doorway to the sink, turned on the cold water and bent over the basin. Cupping the water in his hands, he splashed it on his face and neck. The sudden shock of the icy water on his burning skin took his breath away, but it brought him back to his senses. He slurped a couple handfuls, momentarily quelling his cough and cooling the fire in his throat.

Harold slowly straightened up and looked in the mirror above the sink.

The thing staring back at him from the other side of the glass wore a ghastly Halloween death mask. Below his sweaty, matted hair his complexion was sallow, grotesque, his lips like two bloodless gray slugs. Harold looked away.

In the living room, the phone rang, startling him. He caught his breath. This prompted another coughing fit, and he leaned over the sink, hacking horribly, deeply, feeling as if his lungs were being ripped apart.

Then something broke loose in his chest and he hawked up a thick clot of blood into the sink. Breathless, he looked down. It was amazingly red against the white porcelain. As he watched with distaste, the viscous lump slowly leached toward the drain. Harold, who had always been squeamish, stared stupidly into the basin, slack-jawed. Coughing up blood was not good. Not good at all.

He wanted very much to return to the refuge of his couch, but he didn't trust his rubbery legs to carry him there just yet. He stood gripping the sink's edge like the safety bar of a plummeting rollercoaster car.

After the fourth ring, the answering machine picked up, and he heard the gruff voice of Big Bud Carver, proprietor of Carver Chevrolet of San Diego, whose motto was *At Carver Chevrolet, we carve the prices to the bone for YOU*.

"Rise and shine, cupcake," he barked, and Harold could see him now, a mountain of flab squeezed behind a titanic pine desk, his immense bulk testing the limits of the suit he wore like an overstuffed sausage stretching its casing—or in Big Bud's case, like three hundred pounds of shit in a two hundred pound bag.

Harold heaved a sigh and closed his eyes.

"You're really putting us behind the eight ball today, buddy boy," Carver continued. "You know damn good and well this is one of the biggest sales of the year, and *you call in sick?* That takes a set of cojones, son, and we both know that is a particular commodity you don't possess. But I'll tell you what you're going to do…" He shifted down into a cold, flat voice, one so utterly devoid of any human feeling that it seemed as if a dead man were talking on Harold's machine. "You're going to grow a pair. Pronto. As in right fucking now. You're going to shake it off, clean it up and get your sorry ass in here. I want you on the lot in an hour." Then he was bellowing again in his usual glad-handing manner, employing that patented tone exclusively reserved for car salesmen and politicians. It was the voice of a man accustomed to getting what he wanted. "We need all hands on deck, son. Chop chop."

There was a loud clatter as the phone slammed down on the other end.

He called me son, Harold thought, feeling more sickened by that little detail than he'd been by the glob of blood oozing toward the drain. *The sonofabitch actually called me son.*

Truth was, once upon a time—up until a year ago, in fact—Harold had been Bud Carver's son-in-law.

Near the end of his senior year in high school, Harold went to a pre-graduation party. Not being part of the popular crowd—or any crowd, for that matter—he was loathe to go. He just wasn't good with people. But his stepfather, Dan, an oafish, insufferable bore, had bullied and badgered him after "overhearing" Harold confess his trepidation to his mother, who was his only ally, albeit a poor one. Dan the Man, alias the Crude Dude (Harold was careful never to utter this epithet out loud) was quite vocal in his view that Harold wasted far too much time with his nose buried in one book or another. And when it came to the boy's love of story writing, Dan was more than generous with his snide comments about what he called his stepson's "scratching and scribbling" which he seemed to take as a personal affront.

Harold was just like his mother: meek, tame, taciturn. He was no match for Dan's sheer doggedness, and in the end, as always, Harold surrendered.

Which was how he found himself in the middle of a crowd of raucous teenagers, sipping his first cold beer ever and feeling overwhelmed by loud music and drunken laughter. And how he lost his virginity to a pretty senior named Christina Carver. She was brash, outgoing, as ebullient as he was reserved. And for reasons he could not fathom, she seemed to like him.

At first, she terrified Harold, but somewhere after his third or fourth beer, the world softened around the edges and he lost his inhibitions in an alcoholic haze. He opened up to her, blathering on about whatever came to mind, uncertain and unconcerned whether anything he said even made sense. It felt wonderful. At some point she began kissing him deeply, hungrily, her tongue exploring the inside of his mouth like . . . well, like the way he wanted to explore the inside of her. His penis grew so engorged it ached, and when she tickled his ear with the insistent whisper, "Fuck me," he thought he would ejaculate then and there.

They wound up in one of the bedrooms. It was awkward, clumsy. Then just like that, it was over.

Three months later she told him he'd knocked her up. Her words.

When Harold thought about it, he realized that his whole life consisted of a series of compromises. He had been coerced and cajoled into every major decision he'd ever made because of his weakness. Afraid of what people would think, how they might react. He fared no better this time. The Crude Dude browbeat him into "doing the right thing." As did Christina's father. A month later Harold and Christina were standing up at City Hall and mumbling marriage vows beneath Big Bud's shadow. After that, it was just a hop, skip, and a jump to a job at Carver Chevrolet. Harold hated himself for succumbing to Big Bud on that score. He wasn't cut out to be a salesman, had neither the talent nor the temperament for it. At first, he continued to write in his spare time, both at home and at work. But it seemed the powers that be had other plans for him. Christina nagged him incessantly about it, saying he needed to quit dreaming and grow up. If he wanted a hobby, why didn't he take up golf, like a normal guy?

And when they got wind of it at the dealership, it was open season. All day long it was, "Yo, Shakespeare, you got a customer." Or, "Hey, Hemingway, they need you upstairs." Some joker even planted a copy of *Writing Fiction for Dummies* on his desk. Then Big Bud collared him in the showroom one afternoon and, with a meaty hand clamped on his shoulder like a vise, told him he had better get his mind right. Harold stopped writing at work. And finally, quit writing at home too.

Then came the miscarriage, which made his and Christina's life together feel even more bleak and pointless than before. That winter, Harold fantasized about disappearing, a couple of times actually cruising by the Greyhound station on his way to the dealership, but then Christina came down with the flu and was laid up for nearly three weeks. She hated being sick more than anything in the world. She was a needy, thankless patient whom no amount of nurture could mollify. When Harold was out of her sight, she howled for his attention. When he was present, she barked at him for hovering. Yet the act of administering to her enveloped Harold in a kind of inertia that somehow kept him from leaving.

Later, when he really let himself think about it, he realized there had been clues all along into Christina's character that should have raised some red flags: her disdain of homeless people, for one. Her blatant disgust of anyone physically or mentally disabled, for another. But the most shocking glimpse into her psyche came on the afternoon they were at the Coffee Bean. And by then, things were mostly over between them anyway.

It was Saturday, September 22, 2001, and they'd been married almost two years to the day. They had been sitting at one of the little tables, she with her usual cappuccino, him with a cup of green tea. Harold never drank coffee; he was nervous enough as it was. Around them, the place buzzed with conversation, but the two of them scarcely acknowledged each other. She was flipping through some glamour magazine while he sat completely immersed in a Ray Bradbury novel.

Then she said, "What's with people?"

Harold looked up absentmindedly. "Hmmm?"

Christina glared at him. "Put that silly book down and pay attention to me."

"Okay," he said, placing the paperback on the table. "I'm all yours."

She rolled her eyes. Then she cast a furtive glance in the direction of the older couple sitting at the next table. She lowered her voice: "Listen."

He didn't like eavesdropping on a conversation, but if he refused he would risk incurring Christina's wrath, so he reluctantly complied, pretending to admire an art nouveau print on the wall. And at once realized that the discussion at the adjacent table concerned the recent events of 9/11.

Harold looked evenly at his wife. "So?" he said.

She returned his look with one of irritation, then leaned in and whispered, "Don't you get it? Everyone's so broken up about that day. I'm sick of hearing about it. What's it have to do with us, anyway? I mean, it's not like it happened here. It was way out there in New York, am I right? So who cares?"

Harold was stunned.

"Tina," he said slowly, "you don't really . . . I mean, you can't—"

"Daddy feels the same way," she said, lifting her chin in a haughty, I-don't-care-what-you-think manner. "I've heard him say so lots of times."

In that moment, Harold understood what he had married.

After the miscarriage, Christina had turned increasingly cold—not that she'd ever been exactly warm in the first place. Two years dragged by. Then she started dropping by the dealership more often, and Harold noticed her making eyes at Joe McKinney, Carver Chevrolet's new salesman and the football hero from their high school days. Harold wasn't surprised when she filed for divorce. He was mortified, however, to see them together right there under his nose, and evidently with Big Bud's approval.

But after a while, he learned to swallow it, like he did everything else. Some would say that accepting something like that, that living with it, would take enormous strength. In Harold's case, they would be wrong.

He stayed at Carver Chevrolet because, the economy being what it was, finding another job wasn't the easiest thing to do. At least that's what he told himself. He also told himself that whatever doesn't kill you makes you stronger. But deep down Harold knew better. He knew he would always be weak, always afraid.

Harold opened his eyes and looked into the sink. His first thought was that his fever was causing him to hallucinate because what he was seeing was impossible.

The glob of blood was creeping upward. As he watched in dismay, it crawled snaillike toward the rim of the sink, leaving a slimy pink trail behind. He saw that the lump was throbbing now as if it had a pulse, a beating heart.

Harold stood straight up, a sound of revulsion escaping his lips. He took two involuntary steps backward.

The glop appeared at the sink's edge, then sat there pulsating. It raised itself up, elongated, stretching like warm taffy toward the ceiling. That's when the very top part of its amorphous form twisted to the right, and he saw a pair of black dots, like two tiny drops of oil, swivel in his direction. Eyes.

Harold turned to run, but he had backed up beyond the half-open bathroom door and, in his blind attempt to flee, he collided with it, slamming it shut. The sudden impact bounced him backward and knocked him to the floor. He lay there on the cold hard tile in a daze, his head cocked at an angle against the side of the bathtub. Then his eyes rolled toward the sink, and terror tore at him with razor-sharp claws.

The thing was now a foot tall. As Harold gaped in horror, it expanded incredibly in height and breadth until it overflowed onto the floor in a gelatinous mass. There it raised itself from a crouch, seeking its full girth, its swollen, pulsating body quickly dominating the small space. In no time at all, the monster had grown to a towering stature, eight feet or more, the bathroom's low ceiling forcing it to hunch over considerably. It loomed over Harold's cowering form, regarding him with large spider's eyes.

Then a gaping maw opened up below those eyes, and a hideous, bloodcurdling shriek issued from its depths.

The better to eat me with, Harold thought, and his mind was swept away.

The thing leaned in and gobbled Harold up in a single gluttonous gulp, then rose slightly and turned toward the mirror. It let out a huge belch.

As it stood gazing at itself in the glass, its nebulous body began to shrink and shrivel. It altered itself in shape and color until it had taken the form of the man it had just consumed.

The thing that had ridden an asteroid to this planet, the very asteroid that destroyed the dinosaurs, stood naked before the mirror, a ravenous grin stretching across its new face. It had slept for millennia but had recently awakened and begun to spread its seed across this world. Part of the process involved absorbing the memories of its host bodies, and this time was no exception.

Harold felt wonderful. He felt hungry. Most of all he felt strong. There was no fear whatsoever, and he wondered what he'd ever been afraid of to begin with. He grinned that voracious grin and asked his reflection, "Who's the Crude Dude now?"

He began to make plans. First, he thought he would get dressed, then head on down to Carver Chevrolet, where they carved the prices to the bone for YOU. Yeah. And once he got there, he thought he might just carve Big Bud to the bone with a nice sharp butcher's knife. Of course, cutting through all that blubber to get to the bone would be a messy job, but it would be a labor of love. Oh yeah. And when he was finished with that, he thought he might pay his ex-wife and her new hubby a little visit.

And give them the flu.

THE MESSENGER

The crowd gathered on Main Street under a brilliant blue sky. It was the first Saturday in April, and the entire town of Cutter Creek had turned out for the event. Vendors, trailed by gaggles of young children, made their way through the throng, peddling cotton candy, hot dogs, and soda pop. The general atmosphere was one of frivolity, and the crowd fairly buzzed with anticipation.

In the middle of the street, a stage had been erected. Upon that sat a microphone on a stand. A murmur rose through the assemblage as Mayor Lunt hauled his three-hundred-plus pounds up the side stairs and mounted the platform. He tapped the mike and a high-pitched teakettle squeal emitted from the PA system, causing many in the crowd to grimace and cringe. Roses bloomed on Lunt's plump cheeks as he grinned down at his constituents.

"I—" he croaked, producing another short burst of feedback. He cleared his throat, blotted beads of sweat from his forehead with a bright white handkerchief, then began again, his thundering voice rolling across the sea of upturned faces. "I've been informed that the procession will be here soon. I'd like the present participants to come up onstage if you will."

At the mayor's behest, three men—Mike Dawes, Kevin Dill, and DeWayne Vance—filed up the steps and onto the stage. Vance carried a large red toolbox.

"Are you gentlemen ready?" Lunt asked them.

All three nodded grimly.

The mayor addressed the townspeople. "How about you folks? Ready for the show?"

The crowd erupted in approval. Colorful streamers arced through the air, noisemakers blasted, and several people gave shrill whistles. As if on cue, the sound of a snare drum rolled across the square, followed by brassy notes and cymbal crashes. Then here they came— the Cutter Creek High School Marching Hatchets down Main Street, resplendent in their blue and white uniforms, playing "The Stars And Stripes Forever."

The crowd went crazy.

The band circled around behind the assembly, which turned almost as one to follow its progress. That is until everyone saw what was bringing up the rear of the procession. Harley Durst's shiny black Ford F150 rolled slowly along behind the ranks of musicians, old Harley himself at the wheel. But that wasn't what drew the crowd's attention. In the pickup's open bed, lashed to the light bar crucifixion style, was Janet Ames, the local writer. She was still wearing the slacks and chambray shirt she'd been arrested in two days ago, and her gray-streaked hair looked knotted and dirty. She stared wildly back at the crowd.

When they reached the foot of the stage the band changed formation, compressing into a tight rectangle as they brought the song to a triumphant finish.

A hush fell over the crowd. Even the small children and babies had fallen silent. In those few mesmerizing seconds the only sound was Harley's truck engine rumbling softly near the stage.

Mayor Lunt broke the spell by booming into the microphone, "How 'bout those Hatchets, huh? Give 'em a hand, folks!"

They did, but their enthusiasm was dampened now. Or rather refocused. As Harley shut off the truck's engine all eyes rolled toward the woman with her arms spread wide, ropes holding her fast to the light rack.

Now Janet Ames raised her voice over the crowd. "What's wrong with you people? How can you let this happen?"

There was no reply, other than Mike Dawes and Kevin Dill tramping down off the stage to the truck. They opened the tailgate and climbed into the bed, then proceeded to untie her. Harley didn't offer to help, opting instead to remain in the driver's seat, where he leaned back and lit up a smoke. Once Janet was unfettered, Dawes and Dill led her to the rear of the truck, then jumped down and offered to help her down as well. Janet gave a humorless laugh and leapt neatly to the street. A few of the townspeople cheered this move, a couple of them even applauding. A murmur rose in the crowd again as the two men escorted her onto the stage.

When they were assembled and all eyes were trained on them, Lunt proclaimed theatrically into the microphone, "Janet Ames, you have been found guilty of debauchery. Have you anything to say for yourself before sentence is carried out?"

Janet shook loose of Dawes and Dill and stepped up to the mike. "This is insane. All I did was write a story. Eugene Morris is the one who actually did those things to those little girls up in that cabin."

This was met with shouts of "Pervert!" and "Shame on you!"

"Shame on me? Shame on *me?*" Her eyes frantically searched the crowd, until they found a young couple about midway back. "You," she hissed. "Steve Mathews. Everybody knows you've been cheating on Jenny, there, screwing little Deanne Carter in that stockroom of yours after you close up the grocery store every night."

Closer to the stage, Deanne Carter gave a horrified squeal and covered her face with her hands. Steve and Jenny Mathews shared a stunned glance, then stared at their shoes. The crowd grumbled, and someone shouted, "Shut your filthy mouth!"

But Janet was scanning the mob again. When her eyes fell on a mountainous man with wild red hair and beard to match, she jerked the mike from its holder and growled, "And you, John Fletcher." The man's icy blue eyes narrowed and his upper lip curled. Beside him stood nine-year-old Henrietta, his daughter and only other occupant of Casa de Fletcher since John's wife had been taken by ovarian cancer three years ago. Henrietta went white as Mayor Lunt's handkerchief, mortified that her father should be suddenly singled out like this. It made the angry bruise on her cheek stand out all the more. Then her face flushed as red as her hair.

"We all know you like to use your little girl as a punching bag whenever you're off the wagon, John," Janet said. Fletcher began to make an animal sound deep in his throat. "But we can't mention those things in polite society anymore, can we? Janet continued. "I just wonder what else you're going to start doing to your daughter."

Fletcher roared like a bear as he surged wild-eyed toward the stage. It took four men to restrain him, and it took several seconds to calm him down, though he stood huffing and snorting and glaring at Janet with murder in his eye.

"We can't talk about anything anymore." Janet's voice rolled across the tide of angry faces. "And we sure as hell can't write about it, either. That's why the *Cutter Creek Gazette* only publishes inoffensive bulletin board announcements since the Change." She fixed Lunt with a hateful gaze. "And why they would never report that our good mayor here has been embezzling funds from the town treasury for over a year now."

The crowd gasped. From his place on the stage, Lunt gave an indignant harrumph, then stormed across the stage and, with hammy hands, wrestled the microphone from Janet's grip. For a moment he appeared ready to bludgeon her with it. But this didn't stop Janet. She raised her voice to the crowd.

"Oh, we know that one day soon he'll be quietly ushered out of office and replaced with new blood, but we won't be able to mention it. Not in public anyway.

"You all kept quiet about what Eugene Morris was doing up in that cabin of his. And you never talk about the day he was—" she gave a sardonic laugh—*"reprimanded* in this very spot by the regulators, though I bet some of you folks took a bloody stone home with you as a souvenir."

A wave of booing and hissing washed over her. Lunt was calling for Dawes and Dill to take her in hand.

Janet shouted over them all. "But New York and California are still free zones, which means my book is going to see the light of day, whether you people like it or not!"

More retorts of "You awful woman!" and "Burn in Hell!" The mayor's two volunteers each seized an arm.

"Maybe I will," Janet Ames answered, her eyes already full of hellfire, "but I'll have plenty of company."

The crowd erupted into a seething, clamorous mass. Several townsfolk launched rotten vegetables at the stage, which struck both Janet and her holders impartially.

Lunt yelled, "Get on with it!"

Dawes and Dill dragged Janet backward while DeWayne Vance produced a pair of pliers from the red toolbox. Janet's screams were hideous. Moments later, her tongue was tossed into the mob. Next

Vance pulled out a small cordless chainsaw. With a rip and a roar, Janet's hands tumbled end over end into the waiting crowd.

It became unspeakable.

Somewhere near the end, Janet stopped screaming.

Then the townspeople of Cutter Creek, satiated and stainless, returned to their homes and hearths to eat dinner, watch television, and sleep the sleep of the just.

DEADFALL LANE

No one else saw what happened that night between me and my wife out behind the shed under a full white moon. No one heard anything, either. Old Harlan Davis lives within shouting distance, but he's deaf as a post and about half blind to boot. Besides, he's crazy as a loon. Bill Pritchard says he was driving by Harlan's house one day and saw him sitting on his porch eating night crawlers out of a coffee can, which I don't doubt for a minute. That leaves our other neighbors, all of whom are pretty remote, and a good three-mile empty stretch of road that runs between the little town of Owensville, Indiana, and our place. The locals call that stretch Deadfall Lane, unofficially renamed from Cutters Lane after the big storm in '05 wiped out much of the woods running along it.

The place I'm speaking of is a twelve-acre parcel of land that's been in my family for three generations. Four, if you count my three-year-old son, Chris. I've never worked the land (don't have the knack or the inclination), but for the last few years I've leased it to Milo Harper, a local farmer, so we've always got by all right.

Beyond our back door and catty-corner to the house is a hutch where I raise rabbits for meat. Overlooking the rabbitry is a gigantic sycamore. The great tree shrouds the outbuilding in its enormous shadow every late afternoon when the sun drops toward the western woods. Or at least it did before things went bad.

I spent a lot of time in that tree as a kid, playing Tarzan, or Robinson Crusoe, or whatever. I've always imagined my own son doing the same. But that won't happen now, because everything changed when the tree started dying.

So I've been sitting on the back porch in the relative cool of the evenings (it's the beginning of September, so the worst of the damnable summer heat has passed), watching the tree wither and waiting for my wife to come back from wherever it is she went.

I said everything changed when the tree began to die, but really it all started when my wife Deb came home stinking of stale beer and a man's cologne late one night about two weeks ago and said she was leaving me for Greg Noffsinger, a local shitbird who poured drinks at Busters in town. And if you want the honest truth, I'd have to say it started long before that. She was bored, she said, and couldn't take living with me even one more day.

I'd suspected for some time, but still, it was hard to hear it out loud like that. Funny, the things a man won't admit to himself, the things he'll go right on living with, like a stone in his shoe.

Standing there in our stifling little kitchen amid the ghost smells of coffee and bacon grease, I started to holler at her. But then I caught myself. I looked down the hallway just off the kitchen, where Chris slept behind a closed door.

I turned back to her. "Deb," I said evenly, "you can't do this."

She brushed past me and reached for her cigarettes on the kitchen table. Plucked one out of the pack and lit it with a bright red Bic. She took a deep drag, raised her chin and blew a stinking cloud of smoke and beer breath in my face. "You can't stop me, Pete," she said.

It turned out she was wrong about that.

I stormed out of the house to keep from putting a fist in her smirking face and went to the shed to tend the rabbits, something that ordinarily soothes me. What happened instead was I stewed the whole time. And the heat wasn't helping matters. It was still August then, and even at night (as anyone from this part of the country can tell you) the humidity clings to you like a second skin. You either learn to live with it or it drives you batshit. The heat sharpened the ripe tang of rabbit dung and stung my nostrils, which only aggravated me further.

I was just finishing up, tugging the chain hanging from the naked bulb over my head and plunging the shed into darkness, when Deb appeared at the open doorway in a wedge of moonlight. It made her bare shoulders look pale as milk and shone through her thin cotton dress, outlining her shape underneath as she stood with her legs slightly splayed. She gripped her battered brown suitcase with three right fingers, resting it against her thigh. The index finger was hooked around our truck's brass key ring. She looked like a gunslinger fixing to draw her trusty six-shooter. Behind her, waiting patiently in the turnaround dirt drive, was her swaybacked nag—our dusty old Ford pickup.

Not a breeze blew, and an orchestra of crickets filled the muggy air with their incessant night song.

I gave her a sidelong look. "You're not taking the truck."

"You can pick it up tomorrow, Pete." She teetered to one side, the suitcase throwing her off balance.

"Why doesn't *he* come fetch you?"

She gave an exasperated sigh. "Why don't you—" she jabbed her left finger at me, and this time she tottered the other way— "get off my back and stop being a pain in the ass?"

I had a vision then. I saw myself throwing her to the ground. Hiking that dress up. Tugging her white cotton panties aside. Then giving her question real meaning. Sweat trickled down my sides and plastered my t-shirt to my back. I slapped at a mosquito on my neck. The maddening trill of the crickets rose on the still air until I thought I might be suffocated by the sound.

"Well, what if I need it?" I said. "What if Chris gets sick or something and—"

"What the hell are you talking about?" she said, looking at me as if I'd just said I wanted to lay her mother. "I'm taking Chris with me."

I smiled at this—I couldn't help it, it was just so absurd—but the smile melted away quick enough. I looked at her. Her words kept echoing in my head until they became utter nonsense. Finally, I found my voice.

"I don't think so," I said. I started to add, not in your condition. But I knew I wasn't about to let her take Chris under *any* condition, so instead, I said simply, "No. You're not."

She looked at me the way someone might look at dog shit on the bottom of their shoe and turned away with a snort of disgust, and I heard her mutter the words, "Watch me."

Something inside me snapped. I was furious and frightened at the same time, and all at once my head was hurting so bad I thought it would explode. The drone of the crickets amplified in my brain. My feet started moving under me, carrying me across the dirt floor. A tiny voice in the back of my mind asked me what the hell I thought I was doing. But it was shouted down by a much louder voice, this one screaming at the top of its lungs, *You dirty stupid fucking whore I hate your rotten stinking goddamn guts.*

That's when I saw the shovel leaning against the inside of the door. It was a brand new Blue Hawk straight from the hardware store in town, its blade gleaming dully in the half-light. I snatched it up as I exited the shed, wrapping my fingers around the logo stenciled along the handle. Stepping up behind her, I yelled, "Hey!"

Deb whirled on her heels, a look of pure surprise in her dark brown eyes. Raising the shovel with both hands, I thrust its business end at her. Only she stumbled as she spun, the drunken bitch, causing me to miss my mark—her shoulder—by a mile. As it was she caught a glancing blow to her right cheek. But glancing or not, the shovel took a nice little bite out of her. Blood brimmed from the fresh gash and flowed down her white jawline, looking like black ink on alabaster in the tricky light. Deb dropped her suitcase and the keys went flying into the air as she clapped a hand over the wound. She looked down in astonishment as the blood continued down her forearm and then brought her eyes up to meet mine. I guess what she saw there sobered her up pretty quickly because she let out an earsplitting scream.

I cringed and threw a frightened glance at the house, at Chris's darkened window. A fan was set in it, its humming blades circulating the hot air in his room. I wondered briefly if its vibration was loud enough to mask what sounded to me like an air raid siren, and doubted it. If Chris woke, all he had to do was sit up in bed and look past the whirring fan blades to the scene unfolding not fifty feet beyond his window. Deb began to backpedal. She started to turn away, but her terrified eyes stayed glued to mine. She was still shrieking. I had to do something.

I drove the shovel's blade straight at her throat, giving it all I had. It went in a good three or four inches, severing her windpipe with a wet *tsssnnk* sound and effectively cutting off her scream. Deb stumbled backward, free of the shovel's blade, and in the space of a heartbeat, I caught a glimpse of the hideous gash two inches below her chin. It looked like a gaping fish's gill. Then her hands flew to her throat, clasping, groping, but they couldn't staunch the sudden horrible glut of blood that was already soaking the front of her dress. Like the blood on her cheek, it looked black in the moonlight. She gawped at me as a grotesque gurgling sound issued from the deep cavity in her throat. I stepped back and watched in morbid fascination as she shuffled back and forth, hacking and retching. A sickening coppery tang filled the air.

I'm not sure how long I stood there in a trance. It seemed like forever, but it couldn't have been more than a few seconds. Then suddenly I shook myself. I looked down at the shovel, cried out and cast it away as if it were a rattlesnake. I wiped my hands on my shirt. Then I slowly raised my head to look at Deb's face once again. Her eyes had become cloudy and stupid. But even as I watched, that vacant look shifted and something began to surface there as if from the depths of a muddy lake. When it swam into focus I moaned and shrank back from it. Her eyes regarded me with a coldness I don't much like to think about. They were the sharp merciless eyes of a crow marking a particularly tasty splatter of sunbaked road kill.

Then she pitched forward on her face in the dirt. Her right leg shuddered in a fitful spasm as she released one last burbling breath. After that, she lay completely still.

In the ensuing silence, I noticed the chirr of the crickets once again. Had they stopped while I was killing my wife? I didn't know.

I hurried up to the house to make sure Chris was still asleep. He hadn't moved a muscle. In the kitchen, I downed an ice-cold can of beer. I blasted cold water into the sink and held my head under the faucet for a few seconds. Then I combed my hair with my fingers and dried my face with a dirty dishtowel.

I went back to check on Deb. Like Chris, she hadn't moved a muscle. I stood there in the sapping heat and looked down at her for a while, then looked up at the bloated white moon. I told myself that I'd had no choice, that her screaming would have roused the boy. But, of course, I'd had it in my mind to kill her the second I picked up the shovel. Because she'd meant to take my son away from me, and I wasn't about to let that happen.

I buried her with her suitcase under the sycamore tree and told everybody she left me. Given the rumors surrounding her and Noffsinger (you can't hide much in a small town) and despite the fact that she never reached him, most folks bought my story. I say most, because murder is a bad business, and I doubt that too many people get away with it completely clean. Deb's folks, who had never forgiven me for stealing away their only daughter, called every day with questions and thinly veiled accusations. Got so I just quit answering the phone. Greg Noffsinger blamed me outright. Pulled his Camaro right up into my driveway two days after Deb went missing, stood in my dooryard, drunk as Cooter Brown, and called me out. He had second thoughts when I stepped out onto my porch with my twelve gauge shotgun cradled in my arm. Fuck him, anyway.

Then there was Tom Harvey, the local sheriff. He paid me a visit late one afternoon while I sat on the back porch, smoking a cigarette, Chris playing with his toy cars at my feet. Tom unfolded his lanky form from his cruiser and ambled up to the steps.

"How ya doin', Pete?" he said, cocking his hat back and letting the sun shine on his homely face.

I gave him a wan smile. "Well as can be expected."

"Yeah," Tom said, and scratched pensively under the hat at his forehead, "about that. Is Deb around? I'd like to speak with her if that's okay."

"You and me both," I said, "but she lit out a few nights ago."

"Is that right?" His eyes searched mine.

"Yeah," I said. My throat was dry all of a sudden, and I needed to swallow. I tried to conceal my bobbing Adam's apple by moving to crush out my cigarette in the dented tin ashtray on the patio table beside me.

"Pete, I'm here on account of Greg Noffsinger's raisin' ten different kinds of hell around town. He's sayin' there've been some goings on out here. Now, normally I couldn't care less what that rummy is spoutin', but it's my job to check it out. And well, there's been rumors…" He trailed off, looking at his boots. Chris rescued him by offering one his toy cars, what looked to me like a black hearse, and Tom took it and tousled my son's cornsilk hair. The sheriff rolled the car distractedly over and over between the balls of his thumbs and his long fingers. A pianist's fingers, I thought.

"It's okay, Tom," I said. "Fact is, Deb was stepping out on me. We had a blowup a few nights ago, and she walked out. I just assumed she was with Noffsinger."

Tom looked up at me again.

"That is," I added, "until he showed up here the other day."

"Yeah," Tom said. "He told me about that. Said you threatened him with a shotgun."

I was already shaking my head. "I just happened to be cleaning it at the time. And he was piss drunk."

Tom nodded. "What else is new?"

There was an uncomfortable silence, and Chris filled it by humming a tuneless song as he trundled his cars about.

"I know how it looks, Tom."

Tom waved it off. "I'm sure Deb will come on home after she cools down. Her folks live in Tennyson, ain't that right? You figure she went there?"

"No," I said, and left it at that. I felt my hands wanting to fidget and was sorry I'd snuffed my cigarette.

"Well, I wouldn't worry too much. My guess is she'll turn up soon enough."

He put Chris's toy car down among the others. "Tank 'ou," Chris said, and Tom ruffled his hair again.

"Prob'ly be a good idea to stick around," the sheriff said, "in case I need to talk to you again."

"Sure."

"Okay. See ya, Pete."

He started away, then stopped and turned back again. "Oh, one more thing. Why didn't you call me when you found out Deb wasn't with Greg Noffsinger?"

I shrugged. "I don't know. I suppose I figured it was like you said, that she'd come home once she cooled off."

Tom looked at me, and I could see he knew I was lying. Then he nodded. "Yeah, I thought so."

He climbed into his cruiser and drove off. He came back only once, but it had nothing to do with my wife's disappearance. By then, Greg Noffsinger had blown town, and the general agreement was that he had finally met up with Deb somewhere. Tom showed up at my place two weeks later, along with the EMTs, because of what happened to Chris.

It was the tree. Six days after I planted my wife beneath it (two days after Tom's visit), I noticed the big sycamore was leaning conspicuously away from the shed, as if trying to distance itself from what happened there. That tree is a hundred years old if it's a day, and for as long as I can remember it's stood straight and tall. There was no earthly reason for it to suddenly start tilting like that.

It tipped further every day. It inclined toward the setting sun, so it should have been casting an eastward shadow. And because of the tree's increasing angle, that shadow should have been shrinking, receding toward the trunk. But against all natural law, it was instead lengthening. At the same time, it crept across the yard like the hour hand of a clock, stealing ever closer to the porch, where I sat waiting. This is impossible, I know. Still, it was happening. That shadow was pointing at me. Reaching for me.

Chris had started crying for Deb at night, and I took to rocking him to sleep. Then I sat on the porch, facing the tree with my shotgun across my lap, and slept with one eye open. I spent the days grainy-eyed and groggy. I couldn't eat, and I stopped bathing, and so I started to get pretty sour. Even Chris wrinkled his nose when I got close.

I was cracking up.

One morning, I decided enough was enough. I knew my wife was coming back for me, and I wasn't going to be there when she showed up. Maybe I deserved what I got, but I still wasn't going to let her take my son. I threw some of our clothes in a suitcase, grabbed the three hundred in cash that I'd secreted away in a box of shotgun shells, then called Milo Harper, the farmer who leased the land from me.

Milo answered after the second ring. "Yep?"

"Milo, it's Pete Denning."

"Hey, Pete, what can I do ya for?"

"You still interested in buying my place?"

There was a moment's hesitation, then he said, "Well, sure, if the price is right."

"It will be. But Milo, the thing is, I'd like to wrap this up today. This morning. I can meet you at the bank on my way out of town."

"Kinda sudden, ain't it?"

I waited.

"Well, uh … yeah, that sounds fine, I suppose. Nine o'clock okay?"

"Sure," I said. "I have a few personal things—not much—that I'll send for later. And you'll need to start taking care of the rabbits right away."

"Sure, sure," Milo agreed.

"And Milo…"

"Hmm?"

"You'll need to cut down the sycamore out back. It's dying."

"Oh, that's too bad."

"Yeah."

I doubted Milo would accidentally uncover Deb's body even if he should pull the stump out of the ground; I'd buried it deep, and far enough out that the unearthed roots shouldn't exhume it. That's what I told myself, anyway. And besides, I had no other choice. I had to chance it. Whatever happened, Chris and I would be long gone by then.

The second I hung up the phone, I called out to Chris. He didn't answer, so I went into his bedroom. He wasn't there. I returned to the kitchen on my way to the living room and hollered, "Son?" Then my eye caught movement through the kitchen window overlooking the back porch and beyond. Chris was standing under the tree, hands on his knees, watching a squirrel. The squirrel had its tiny paws to its mouth, its cheeks agitating as it munched on a tasty morsel.

I cried out and ran to the screen door, banging it open and fairly leaping over the porch to the backyard. "Chris!" I yelled. The squirrel shot away, and Chris stood up straight and turned toward me, a smile of wonder on his face. *"Kurl,"* he squealed, and above him, I heard a sharp crack, and one of the heavy limbs fell toward the ground. Its thick end struck the top of my son's head, turning it at a right angle and producing another sickening crack as his knees unhinged and his little body crumpled beneath the limb.

Everything seemed to turn upside-down after that. All at once I was above myself, looking down as I rushed without thought to where Chris lay and lifted the limb from his little body and heaved it aside, wrenching my back something awful, though I wouldn't feel it until the next day. I watched myself gently scoop him up and carry him to the house, seeing him swing bonelessly in my arms. I heard myself screaming over and over again, "You can't have him!" I called 911, then sat on the kitchen floor with my broken son in my arms and cried myself hoarse and waited for the ambulance to come.

They tell me it was a nice funeral. I really don't remember. I was on muscle relaxers for my back and everything seems like a foggy gray dream to me now. I think the rabbits have died. I don't know. Hard to say how many days it's been. All I can think about is Chris.

Well…that's not altogether true.

The tree now leans crazily toward the western horizon while its unnatural shadow points directly at me. Its roots are pulling themselves up from the earth on this side, leaving a ragged hole. I try not to think about what sort of awfulness will be born there. The leaves—those that aren't brushing the ground—are shriveling and dropping to the earth like dead brown birds, because the thing that used to be my wife is drawing the life from them, draining them dry the way a vampire drains blood from its host. And when it's done, the tree will fall at last.

Meantime, I've just been sitting on the back porch in the relative cool of the evenings, watching the tree wither and waiting for my wife to come back from wherever it is she went.

WATER AND WAR

The alien sat on the sofa, watching the man at the computer.

"What are you doing?"

"I'm paying my water bill," the man answered.

"Please explain again what is paying."

The man did, and afterwards, the alien laughed in that peculiar chortle which sounded like choking.

"We do not pay for water on my world. It is there for all. You *hoomans* have very perplexing ways."

The alien had been living with the man for a few days now. He'd basically grasped the language in a matter of hours—was, in fact, becoming increasingly proficient every day—though his pronunciation was slightly impeded by his strange palate.

The man lit a cigarette and blew a puff of smoke toward the ceiling. This never failed to bewilder the extraterrestrial, and his featureless face took on an expression which was, after his own kind, one of puzzlement.

"Why do you poison yourself so?"

"It's a bad habit, I know," the man admitted.

"I have observed on your tee-vee that your entire species seems bent on poisoning itself. You travel in crude vehicles which choke the atmosphere with toxins. You knowingly devastate vast realms of your own planet in order to produce a primitive form of energy which, in turn, only serves to poison your world yet further. Why would you do this, when the sun and the wind are at your fingertips?"

"Why do we shit where we eat, in other words," the man said.

The alien looked at him with bright black eyes.

The man sighed. "I guess it comes down to money."

The next morning the man shuffled into the living room in wrinkled pajamas and found the alien sitting on the sofa and flipping through the channels on the television, the remote control poised loosely in his three-fingered hand. His visitor glanced up.

"Ah," he said, "you are conscious. I trust you slept well."

"Fine, thanks." The man didn't ask in turn whether his guest was well rested. He'd discovered that the alien required little or no sleep.

The creature returned his attention to the TV. "I have been learning about money," he said. He shook his head in wonder. "It is baffling to me that you *hoomans* place so much value on such a worthless article of trade."

"It's baffling to me sometimes too," the man said.

"It is reprehensible that those who possess it are allowed to live their lives in comfort, while those who do not must suffer for the want of it."

The man nodded in agreement. "The haves and have-nots," he said. "Probably the main reason for every war that's ever been started." He yawned as he rubbed his stubbly chin. "Have you eaten yet?"

"I was waiting for you," said the alien, his tiny slit of a mouth turning up in a smile.

The man turned toward the kitchen. "I'll make us some breakfast."

The creature watched him go, his smile fading as a shadow fell across his strange face like a cloud passing over the sun.

Two days later, the alien confessed to the man that he was deeply troubled.

The creature was sitting in his usual place on the sofa. The man sat facing him, his back to his desk. He lit a cigarette, then, through a wisp of smoke, said, "What's wrong?"

"War," the alien said, and there was great sadness in his voice. "I never conceived of such a thing before I came here. How could I? There is no word for it in my language. You have many words for violence, and now that I know them, I cannot *unknow* them, though I wish I could. I am not certain whether I will be able to make my people understand the concept upon my return home. Having seen it myself, I am still unable to comprehend it."

Something about what his visitor said—the part about making his people understand—bothered the man, but he didn't know why, exactly. For some reason, he felt guilty.

"It's complicated," he explained, snuffing his half-smoked cigarette in the ashtray on his desk.

"It is not," countered the alien. "It is dreadfully simple. Your species is set upon the path to extinction, a path which you yourselves are clearing. What is so confounding is how a people of such evident intelligence can be so conversely stupid."

This rankled the man somewhat, yet he had to agree with his guest. "I feel the same way you do, but I'm just one man. What can I possibly do to change things?"

The creature looked at him with those bright obsidian eyes and said, "I do not know."

They were both silent for a moment, each alone with his own thoughts. Finally, the man said, "Then what's the point?"

"I have read in your books of history about the teachings of such men as Jesus and Gandhi. These men were very wise, perhaps even transcendent on your evolutionary scale. And there have been others like them. But, unfortunately, individuals such as these seem to be the exception rather than the rule. As a species, I fear you are lost. This thing, this hostility, is like a virus which has infected your whole planet. And there is not much time left. This world is in its death throes."

The next day, the alien entered the kitchen while the man was slicing roast beef for a sandwich.

"I must be leaving soon," said his guest.

The man looked up from the counter and into the creature's huge dark eyes, and immediately felt that inexplicable sense of guilt. "Oh," he said. "Okay."

"You have been most hospitable."

The man shrugged. "It's been no trouble."

The alien looked at the man a moment longer, then dropped his eyes to the scuffed linoleum floor, an act of reticence that made him appear oddly humanlike.

"I feel that we have become friends," he said. "Am I wrong in this assumption?"

"No," replied the man. "We're friends."

Now the creature raised his head and met the man's gaze directly. "I have traveled to many worlds," he said, "and I almost always return to my own people with some new knowledge, knowledge which we incorporate into our society in order to better ourselves, which is our way. Some of these planets have yielded no great results, being that they were desolate or, at best, inhabited by lower life forms. Otherwise, my world has been continually enriched by my visits to planets peopled by intelligent beings . . . Until now. I am at a loss as to how the leaders of my world could possibly make use of what I have seen here. And how can I teach them what I myself do not understand? It is a daunting prospect, and I feel I am not up to the task. But I must make an effort. I regret, however, that in so doing I will be dishonoring your people and, hence, you, who have been so generous to me."

As the alien unburdened himself, a look of dawning realization crept over the man's face, and he stared at his visitor, his friend, with horror-filled eyes. The words of this innocent creature rang in his head. Now he knew why he felt at fault.

But he also knew what he had to do.

"I am sorry," the alien said.

"So am I," said the man, though he meant something else, entirely. Tears sprang to his eyes as he raised the butcher's knife from the kitchen counter.

Two weeks later, the man stood in his backyard, sprinkling water from a plastic pitcher onto his new flower bed. He'd planted yellow and orange California poppies. As he stood admiring their bright burst of colors, he thought about his friend and their parting conversation. He thought about that curious feeling of guilt after the alien spoke of returning to his own people and wondered that he hadn't recognized it for what it was right from the start. In the end, however, it had become all too clear.

A faint breeze stirred the leaves of the Japanese maples, and in their soft murmur he imagined he could hear the quiet voice of his friend:

I am not certain whether I will be able to make my people understand . . . knowledge which we incorporate into our society . . .

how the leaders of my world could possibly make use of what I have seen here . . .

He drained the pitcher, then set it on the grass at his feet. That done, he removed the cigarette that was cocked behind his ear, dug a Bic from his pocket, and lit up. He exhaled his first drag with a long sigh, looking down at the flower bed.

"I couldn't let you take that back with you," he told the poppies.

The man took another pull on his cigarette and recalled one of the last times they had spoken to each other:

I am sad to tell you these things. I do not understand why you hurt yourselves so, why you hurt one another. Still, I see within you a light which seems inextinguishable—that which may yet prove to be your salvation.

What is it? the man had asked.

Hope, answered the alien.

Now the man addressed the blameless blue sky. "Yes," he said, "I suppose there is that."

STONES

Night was falling, but Zach thought he should stay hidden behind the dumpster until full dark. Because they were out there somewhere, and if they caught him he was dead.

He glanced anxiously around the dumpster at the alley's mouth, then drew back. Zach had quickly checked inside the thing for something to eat, but it was as empty as his stomach. So he hunkered in the gathering darkness with only his fear and hate to fill the void.

At the alley's entrance, a gruff voice said, "In here." On the heels of that, a sharp, nasal assent: "Yeah, yeah," followed by a high-pitched giggle. Zach looked frantically about for a weapon and discovered only a flimsy slat from a busted crate. But he gripped the piece of wood in his fist as if his life depended on it—which he knew damn well was true.

The waning daylight left widening pools of shadow around him, and Zach immersed himself in one. Crouching lower, he pressed his back into the rough brick wall.

He heard them kicking debris aside before two figures moved into view. They turned to give Zach's hiding place a quick once-over, but that he should *be* there staggered them. They retreated, eyes widening. Zach rose slowly, evenly, so as not to provoke them. He stole a glance up the alley. There had been four of them. Where were the other two? No matter.

These two looked to be in their late twenties. One big, with greasy dark hair, the other smaller, with a bleached-blond buzz-cut. They struggled to regain their bearings, looking like a couple of befuddled dogs that had actually caught the car they'd been chasing.

"Listen," Zach said, his voice faltering, "I don't want no trouble."

The blond gestured at the slat in Zach's hand. "Then what's that for?"

Zach shrugged. "Just in case."

"We almost had your ass back there," the big one said, "huh, Diz?"

"Yep," said the blond. "Frank and Richie got your pal, though." The word *pal* was said with mockery.

Zach flinched. *Charlie.*

He'd noticed them a block behind him after he left the motel. At first, he didn't give them much thought, until he heard their catcalls as they swung along the sidewalk, getting closer. *Can they tell?* Zach had wondered fretfully, as he so often did when he feared others could see right through him as if he were made of glass. He'd walked faster, breaking out in a cold sweat. They matched his pace. Finally, panicked, he bolted.

They gave chase.

At the time, he'd been too frantic to put it together, but now he realized they must have been passing by and seen that single, loving stroke, Charlie's fingers lightly brushing Zach's cheek as Zach slipped out of the motel room door. And the other two had doubled back to ambush Charlie.

Zach wanted to scream.

"You freaks make me sick," the big one growled, and suddenly the air seemed to crackle with electricity.

They set upon him.

Zach stood his ground. It was beat or get beaten, simple as that. Just like when he was a kid, before escaping the orphanage—and just like it had been ever since, growing up in these slums and dealing with hate his whole life. When he could, he fled. But when he was backed into a corner—like now—his only choice was to fight for that life. Because bad as it was, it was the only one he had.

And besides, now there was Charlie to consider.

As the big one closed in, Zach brought his boot up fast and hard, kicking the dude dead between the legs. There was a solid *thump*. The guy grunted and slumped to the ground like a top-heavy sack of dirt, drawing his knees to his chest, retching. The blond gawked at his downed partner. "Earl?" he said in a small, bewildered voice. Then that look of surprise darkened like a storm cloud as he raised his face to Zach's. "You son of a—"

Zach stabbed him in the eye with the slat. The guy howled, slapping a hand over his face as he stumbled backward and fell. Zach flung the plank away and sprinted toward the street. At the mouth of the ally, he stopped to glance back. The big one was already staggering to his feet. The blond sat up, a hand clamped over his face, one eye glaring at Zach with pure hatred.

He screamed, "We're gonna get you, fucker!"

Zach ran. Past the crumbling tenements and rusted heaps. Past dark empty lots and wary eyes watching from windows. He ran with only one thought bursting in his brain: *Charlie!* But soon a painful stitch in his side made him stop. He bent over, gasping, his throat dry and ragged, his lungs on fire.

Then he heard their voices echoing off the buildings, calling out to him, cursing him. With a desperate sob, he ran on.

At the motel, Zach sprinted to the unit at the far end and slammed his fist against the door. It bounced open, revealing the splintered doorjamb. He rushed inside. "Charlie!" But a quick search proved the room to be deserted.

He hurried back outside, then froze in his tracks.

They were twenty feet away.

But their faces were turned toward each other in conversation. So they hadn't seen him yet. This was Zach's only chance. He began edging along the façade in plain view, praying

they wouldn't notice him. Just as they turned their faces forward, Zach slipped around the corner of the building into solid black shadow. He flattened himself against the wall and felt his heart trying to rip through his chest.

Soon he heard them rummaging through the room behind him.

Then the big one's muffled voice: "He's not here. Let's go."

Seconds later they breezed by Zach, so close he got a whiff of their stink. They crossed the narrow street and headed down the crumbling sidewalk. Zach stayed where he was, watching them go.

Before they got out of earshot, Diz said, "If we'd've had Frank's gun that sonofabitch wouldn't've got away, I'll tell you that."

Zach started after them.

The trip through the dark streets left him completely turned around. His throat was scorched, his empty stomach rumbling in outrage. Finally, he saw them mount the stoop of a derelict house up ahead. They traipsed across the porch and disappeared through the front door. Zach hurried up the street and crouched behind an abandoned car. He looked up at the house, thought about the men inside, and his anger boiled over.

Men like that had made him afraid all his life, had filled him with so much hate that he was sick with it half the time. But worst of all, they had made him ashamed of what he was.

No more.

Zach crept from behind the car and tiptoed alongside the house, keeping low. He circled the entire structure and, failing to find easy ingress, wound up where he started.

He squatted next to a basement window. Gripped the bottom of the pane with his fingertips and tugged. With an obstinate groan, the window swung partially open. He waited in silence for a minute, listening, then poked his head inside. He could make out a ghostly gray light. That was it. Directly beneath the window was pitch blackness.

Zach stretched out on his stomach and inched his body into the aperture feet first. It was an uncomfortably tight fit, and when his chest crossed into the hole, he got completely stuck. He hung there on the edge of panic, totally exposed, the window frame digging painfully into his back. The constraint of the casing was crushing his chest, cutting off his breath. It felt as if the entire house was sitting on top of him. He wriggled and wrenched, straining his muscles, feeling bones wanting to snap. He gritted his teeth and pushed hard with the heels of his hands.

Then something *did* snap—one of the hinges. In a sudden excruciating, back-scraping motion Zach fell through the hole and into space. His hands scrabbled desperately at the rough wall for support before his brain caught up with his feet and he realized he was standing on solid ground. He pressed his clammy cheek against the wall, inhaling must and mildew, and waited for his heart to quit thundering and his breathing to slow down. He turned around on shaky legs and waited for someone to come and investigate the sound of his graceless entry. When that didn't happen he began to survey the darkness.

A wooden stairway descended into the blackness, the wan light from the top fading like a dying gasp halfway down its crooked steps.

He crept to the foot of the stairway. A door stood open at the top. Taking a deep breath, Zach ascended the steps.

He stood in a tiny alcove. From somewhere deeper in the house came faint voices. He leaned forward and peered past the niche into a darkish kitchen. He stepped into it. There was a cupboard above a cluttered counter. He stared at it longingly, wondering if it contained food. No, he didn't dare. The light and the voices came from an L-shaped hallway off the kitchen. Zach searched quickly but quietly through the drawers until he found a rusty

butcher's knife. Wielding the weapon, he proceeded along the hallway. Halfway down, a door stood slightly ajar. With his free hand, Zach gently pushed it open, letting light spill into the room beyond. What he saw there stopped him cold.

Books. Everywhere. Covering the walls, stacked all about the room. He skimmed a thousand titles at once: *David Copperfield, Of Mice And Men, Collected Poems Of T.S. Eliot, The Catcher In The Rye, 1984, Fahrenheit 451,* and so many more. Zach was dumbfounded. He'd seen books before, of course, but never had an inkling there were this many in the whole world.

Sudden shouting shook Zach out of his reverie and he spun in that direction, bringing the knife up. But he instantly realized the angry words weren't directed at him. He crept to the corner, listening. They were right in the next room.

"I say we off this freak." Zach recognized the nasal voice of Diz and, though the statement was foreboding, he silently rejoiced, because it meant that Charlie was still alive. For now, anyway.

"If you don't shut up," came a new, menacing voice, "I'll off *you*."

There was a moment of thick silence. Then Diz said, "Jeez, Frank. I didn't mean nothin'."

"What're we arguing about?" someone else said, and it wasn't the big one, Earl. That left Richie. "They'll give us food for this perv."

"That's the truth," Earl agreed.

Then a fifth voice spoke up, physically frail, but weighty with conviction.

"Truth? What would you know of truth?"

"Edward—" Frank began.

"Quiet," the voice came again. "Shame on you. This is a *human being* you're talking about."

Zach braced himself, then stole a glance around the corner. Five men gathered in a large front room. Plopped down on a ratty sofa were Earl and Diz. They stared at their feet. Closer, two men stood with their backs turned. They regarded an old man who stood before them and certainly would have spotted Zach. But his wizened face was half turned away as he looked sadly at something out of Zach's line of sight. Zach stared at him, fascinated. There weren't that many old people left anymore, and Zach thought that this guy might very well be the oldest person in the world.

He motioned to his left. "These people deserve the right to live their lives just as we do. Why can't you understand that?"

"We've heard all this before," said Frank.

"But have you *listened*?"

Zach craned his neck to see who the old man gestured at—certain it was Charlie—but no luck. What he did see, though, made his jaw drop open. On a wood cabinet farther in the room lay a revolver, bullets winking in its chamber. He stared at it pensively. Trouble was, Zach didn't have a chance in hell of reaching it before they spotted him. He leaned back out of sight. Think, *think!* his mind screamed.

And it came to him. Silently withdrawing, he doubled back to the kitchen and swept his eyes across the countertop until he found what he was looking for among the clutter: a glass salt shaker. Even empty, it was heavy. Then he returned to his place of cover. He risked another peek into the room. They were all just as he had left them, except now the old man was looking down and shaking his head. Perfect. Well, maybe not perfect, but it would have to do.

Stepping from concealment, Zach drew back and, with all his might, hurled the shaker at the front window across the room. It was a long throw, but a good one. In a rising arc, the glass missile flashed across the air and shot through the window with a sharp crash. It had the effect Zach wanted. The room erupted in sudden commotion as everyone rushed to the broken window, assuming the attack had come from outside. Everyone, that was, except the old man. He stood silently watching, a smile playing about his puckered lips, dark good humor twinkling in his intelligent eyes, as Zach went for the gun.

Trading the knife for the revolver, Zach stepped into the room. And there was Charlie, tightly bound to a chair with a length of rope.

When she saw him her face lit up. Zach beamed back at her, overjoyed. Then he noticed her bruised and bloody cheek behind the tumble of auburn hair and his smile twisted into a scowl.

He raised the gun and yelled, "Hey!" They all jumped and whirled around, gaping at Zach in disbelief, which instantly turned to dread when they noticed the gun.

"Sit your asses down on that couch right goddamn now."

They immediately complied.

The old man hadn't moved. He stood smiling at Zach companionably. Keeping his eyes glued to the sofa, Zach asked him to untie Charlie. The old man said he would be delighted. When she was free, Charlie flew to Zach's side.

"You came for me," she whispered. Her hands fluttered over him like birds, reassuring herself that he was real. Tears filled her wide, disbelieving eyes. *"You came for me."*

The old man tossed the bundle of rope aside and settled onto the chair with a sigh.

Zach pulled Charlie protectively against him, all the while glaring at his captives. Diz looked as if he was going to cry or wet his pants, maybe both. Earl and Richie looked appropriately scared. But the one called Frank passed an unhurried hand through his close-cropped dark hair, returning Zach's glare with a defiant smirk, his black eyes dancing with glee.

"Well, you've got the gun," he said. "What's the plan, big man?"

"To kill you, Frank," Zach said evenly. He thought he saw Frank's mouth twitch, but that was all. Diz wailed in anguish. Charlie's arm tightened around Zach's waist.

"Forgive my grandnephew," the old man said, "His father—my brother's son—was taken to the camps soon after Frank was born. I've done my best with him, but my lessons are constantly undermined by the outside world."

"Edward, he don't need to know our business!" Frank protested.

"Hush," the old man said, and Frank leaned back, glowering at the ceiling. Then the old-timer looked at Zach and Charlie consideringly. "Neither of you knew your parents, did you?"

Before escaping to the slums, the only life Zach had ever known was the horror of the orphanage. And he knew Charlie had only a vague memory of being snatched from the arms of a wailing woman who, over the years, had become faceless.

"I thought not," said the old man, as if they'd responded. "It's not sensible to claim a child these days. And naturally, women have no option but to allege they were raped. I'm Edward, by the way."

Zach gave a noncommittal nod, then looked at Frank, who now stared blankly back at him.

"You noticed my library on your way in?" Edward asked Zach.

"Libary?"

"Li*brary,* my boy. A collection of books."

Zach nodded.

Edward eyed him for a moment. "Can you read?"

Zach shrugged. "Some."

"And the young lady?"

Charlie shook her head, causing her hair to spill over the hurt side of her face.

"Most books have been banned for ages, of course. If the authorities discovered mine, I'd no doubt be sent to the camps." Edward heaved a deep sigh as he looked wistfully up at Zach. "But I've never been able to part with a single volume."

Zach nodded toward the couch. "You're not worried about them ratting you out?"

Edward laughed softly. "If that happened, this house would be seized, and those hooligans would be sleeping in the gutter. Besides, it's a moot point. They'll be dead soon, yes."

Diz moaned miserably.

"Why…" Charlie began.

"Yes?" Edward gently urged.

"You're not like them." She nodded toward the couch.

Edward was silent for a time, his eyes glazing over as if he were looking at some impossibly faraway place.

"Things used to be different. You know, there was a time when there was plenty to eat and drink. That's right. Supermarkets filled with anything you could want."

Zach and Charlie exchanged a skeptical look.

Edward chuckled. "I know. It's hard to believe. But it's true. And when I say 'anything', I mean *anything:* Eggs, milk, bread and butter. Meat. Fruits and vegetables. And wine. Oh, *God in heaven*, how I miss wine."

Zach remembered the same stories from the heads of the orphanage; he'd always assumed they were lies.

"And," the old man continued, "in those days people could actually have fresh water pumped directly into their homes with just the *twist of a wrist!"*

This part Zach believed. The useless, rusted metal snouts were everywhere.

"Then we began running out of things. Oh, the warnings had been coming since before I was born, but nobody listened, not really. Not until the wars over food and water started.

"When the electronics failed everything fell apart. Tribes formed. There were riots in the streets, rapes, and murders in broad daylight, and no one to stop it. That's when I began secretly transferring books here from the local library.

"I won't expound on the tribulations of those times. Suffice it to say things were...unpleasant." Edward's face darkened with painful memories.

"In the meantime, the environment was engineering its own effect on children being born across the world. I believe they called it 'natural selection.' Since mankind was depleting the planet's resources at an unsustainable rate, nature simply decided that there should be fewer people. We always assumed some super-virus would reduce our numbers. What began to happen instead was that—and I should think this a fair estimate—around eight out of every ten children born were homosexual."

"Wait a minute," Zach said. "You're saying that heteros—"

"Were the accepted majority, yes. It was the gays—my community—who were persecuted in those days. A great many considered us unnatural, argued that our traits were nothing more than a wrong lifestyle choice." Edward laughed and shook his head. "Do you know that every species on the planet has a homosexual subset? So you see, *nature,* not man, decides what is natural and what is not."

Zach was speechless.

"And so," Edward continued, "a new social order rose from the ashes. But it carried with it a deep and abiding hatred for the ones who'd nearly brought about the end of the world through their gluttony and incessant propagation. And it laid the foundation for the world you now know. Breeding became absolutely forbidden. All heterosexuals were sent directly to the camps for castration or sterilization. Or worse. Of course, children were still being born, because who can identify a breeder on sight? And because, once again, it is evidently nature's intention.

"Finally came 'reeducation,' which was simply the attempted murder of free thinking, of ideas. And books were full of dangerous ideas. So they banned any book that contained even the slightest suggestion of heterosexuality, which was virtually all of them. They kept the Bible, of course—religion pacifies the masses, you know—though not completely intact, striking such phrases as, 'Be fruitful and multiply.' And in the end, they restored stability. Of a sort."

Zach felt dissatisfied, cheated somehow. "So that's it?"

"I don't know," Edward said. "Are you still planning to kill them?"

Zach looked at Charlie's battered profile, then into her questioning eyes. He turned and glared at the watchful men on the couch.

Edward said, "I ask you to consider this: One of them hurt the young lady, and you hurt one of them." He looked at Diz. "An eye for an eye, as it were."

Zach regarded Frank. He imagined putting a bullet between those dark, bright eyes.

"I wonder," Edward went on, "if you've the strength to show them the mercy they weren't prepared to show you. I wonder if you know how much more powerful that would be than all my words combined."

Zach wondered the same thing. But he had Charlie back, and that was all that really mattered, right? His hate was still there, like his hunger, gnawing at his gut. There was no denying it. Question was, could he go on living with it until it ate him up inside? He had no answers. He felt the weight of the world on his shoulders and was suddenly very tired. At last, he said to Charlie, "Let's go," to which she nodded eagerly.

"One moment," Edward said. He rose and brushed past them, disappearing down the hallway. While he was gone, Zach stared evenly at the four men on the couch. They sat unmoving, watching him watch them.

Edward returned with a plastic jug of water, a chunk of bread, and four books. When he presented the bread and jug to Charlie, she shrank away, shaking her head. But after some gentle coaxing, Edward persuaded her to accept them. The books he offered to Zach.

"Best I could manage on short notice," Edward said, "but I think these will do."

Gun in hand, Zach clumsily shuffled the battered books, glancing at the titles: *To Kill A Mockingbird, Anne Frank: The Diary Of A Young Girl, Webster's New World Dictionary,* and a Bible.

Zach looked at Edward questioningly.

"The dictionary is to help you make sense of the words you don't understand," Edward said. Then his rheumy eyes gazed deeply into Zach's. "The others? Well … they're about casting stones."

Zach wasn't sure he understood, but for some reason his eyes welled up with tears. He tried to say thank you but choked on the words.

Charlie suddenly leaned in and awkwardly embraced the old man. "Oh," Edward said, looking pleasantly surprised.

Then he accompanied them to the door. He and Zach looked at each other for a long moment.

Frank, Richie, Earl, and Diz looked on in suspicious silence, Diz with just the one eye.

Then Zach said to them, "It's over." It was all he could think to say.

Zach and Charlie slipped out the door and into the night. They descended the steps, then stole away among the shadows, heading back into the heart of the city. Along the way, they stopped to rest inside an abandoned warehouse. There they ate the bread and washed it down with sparing sips of water from the plastic jug. Then they walked on beneath a dark sky that looked down without comment on a world that had forsaken them long before they were ever born. Zach clutched the books in the crook of his left arm. The gun was in his right hand. He thought about love and hate.

DEATHBED

irplanes and elevators. I abhor them both. And it seemed no sooner had our stressful four-hour flight on the one ended (our brief cab ride through the dark, silent city being my only respite) than we found ourselves being hoisted aloft on the other. I'd left my stomach somewhere over Kansas. Figured I'd pick it up on my way back to California.

I'm not too keen on hospitals, either. Yet here I was in one—indeed, the very one where I'd been born. It occurred to me (not for the first time) that the past is always reaching out to drag us relentlessly back, like a black hole from which even light cannot escape. It was a depressing thought. I squeezed Ellie's hand and she looked up at me with a little wrinkle in her brow.

"It'll be okay," she said, although we both knew it wouldn't.

We were alone in the small space, and I began to feel claustrophobic. My heart started pounding to beat the band and I realized I wouldn't need to retrieve my stomach on the return trip after all. It had tracked me down and was in there now, doing somersaults.

When the elevator doors slid open on the fifth floor and the overwhelming smell of disinfectant (not to mention the underlying stink of sickness and dying) wafted in, it certainly didn't help matters much. We exited the car and followed the signs to the ICU, an enclosed area made up of large-windowed rooms with a nurses' station at its hub.

Hospital workers, some dressed in brightly colored smocks, others clad in green scrubs, bustled about on their various errands. Still clasping hands, my wife and I approached a mid-thirties brunette seated behind a horseshoe-shaped counter, intently tapping away at her computer keyboard. In one of the rooms, I could hear a woman weeping softly.

The brunette looked up at us expectantly, and I was about to ask her which room my father was in when another woman's regrettably recognizable voice said behind us, "So...the prodigal son returns," although she pronounced it *prodijal*.

I looked around and there she was. My stepmother. That feeling I mentioned before about the past being like a black hole engulfed me, and suddenly I was ten years old again and sitting in the back seat of my dad's '65 Mustang. We were at the drive-in, the sun having just dipped below the horizon, and we were waiting for the first picture to start. Don't remember what it was. I do recall Jim Croce's "Bad Bad Leroy Brown" coming from the tinny speaker hooked on the driver's side window. And I remember her turning around in her seat with that smug look on her hatchet face, telling me convincingly, hatefully,

"You'll never fill your father's shoes." My dad had been right there beside her, stuffing his mouth with great handfuls of homemade popcorn from a grease-stained brown paper bag. He never said a word.

Back then my stepmother wore a whorish amount of makeup and cheap perfume, the way some dull-witted women are wont to do. Standing before her now, I still found her scent overpowering, except it had become that sickeningly sweet old lady smell, which joined forces with the other offending odors in the air to really do a number on me. I breathed through my mouth in self-defense. It appeared she'd eased up on the face paint, but that judgmental look still sat perched on her pinched, just-sucked-on-a-lemon face. Her disapproving eye fell on Ellie for a second, then fixed back on me.

"I didn't think you'd show up," she said.

I shrugged. "Guess you were wrong."

"I thought you'd be too busy living the good life out there in California to—"

"Where is he?"

She glared at me, and I wished I had a dollar for every time she'd ever looked at me that way.

"You know," she said, her eyes drilling into me, "you never showed any respect, even as a kid. It's so *flustrating.*"

I was struggling to keep my temper (and stomach) in check.

"Listen," I said, "I don't have time for this. Just tell me what room he's in."

My wife, God love her, stood there holding my hand, not saying a word.

Meanwhile, my stepmother impaled me with a look of pure hatred. That look (along with everything else she had said and done to me over the years) might have hurt, had I ever given half a damn what she thought of me. But you have to care about somebody before they can hurt you in that way, and I never cared for her one lick. My father, on the other hand...

"He's in there," she spat, jerking a thumb over her shoulder, and there was enough venom in her words to bring down a horse. Then she gave a parting shot as we brushed past her: "If he could talk anymore—which he can't—I'm sure he'd ask you why you never call."

We left her standing there in a cloud of her own poison and crossed the ICU to the room where my father lay dying of cancer. Ellie remained at the threshold while I stepped into the dimly lit space beyond.

And there he was. The man who had ruled my world like a towering, mad king...brought low at last. Standing there at the foot of his deathbed, watching his narrow chest rise and fall, in short, shallow breaths, I thought, This is what I was so afraid of? I felt sudden anger well up inside me, and my stomach churned again in disgust at the sight of this weak and withered thing before me. The image of a dried up, dead leaf skittered across my mind, and I shuddered.

Then a flood of unwelcome memories rushed over me: how, when I was twelve, my uncle Jim had been visiting, and at one point had begun casually to flip through a story of mine which I'd left on the coffee table; how he had declared indulgently to me that someday I would be a great writer. And how, to my immense heartbreak and disillusionment, my father had rolled his eyes and countered simply, "I doubt that."

I remembered being shamed into calling his wife my mother. I recalled the routine beatings. The endless, exhausting fear. And the crushing hopelessness, which became my constant companion.

I recalled the year my grade school held its homecoming dance. To my delight and horror, I was voted king, and Julie something-or-other was chosen as my queen. It became the talk of our little town. But my dad balked at the idea of buying me a suit for the occasion. Over the next week, I cajoled and complained. He wouldn't budge. Finally, hours before the event, I lashed out in desperation. This got me banished to my room without supper that night.

For the next month or so everyone at the school (teachers included) shunned me for spoiling the festivities. I could offer only flimsy excuses, being too ashamed of the truth. Of course, it means nothing in the grand scheme of things, but at the time it was a big deal, and I was mortified. I mean, hell, I was just a kid, and the whole damn town was mad at me. Because of him. It was too much to bear. I hated him for putting me through that. And, moreover, for never simply saying he was sorry.

I looked down at what was left of the man I had once been so afraid of, yet had still somehow loved. Now his life was receding like his hairline.

I stepped to the bedside and he opened his eyes. When they finally focused on me, they became shiny with tears and a tired smile touched his lips. I leaned closer to him.

"Can you hear me?" I whispered.

He nodded.

"Good," I said, "because I've got something to tell you, and I want to make sure you understand it. It's this: you were a shitty excuse for a father."

The smile melted off his face like candle wax. He now stared up at me with a mixture of hurt and disbelief.

"That's right," I said. "All those years ago, it wasn't me who wasn't good enough. It was you."

He blinked in amazement, and a tear spilled down his gaunt cheek.

"I just wanted you to know that before you died—that you weren't good enough. Not even close. I'll never visit your grave, wherever that might be. And I promise you this: after I leave you here to rot, I'm going to do my damnedest never to think of you again."

Then I went to the door, took my wife's hand, and we got out of there.

That was two years ago. Other than writing this down, I've kept the oath I made that awful night. Because you should always keep a promise you make to someone on their deathbed.

It's only right.

TO CATCH A FLY

Have you ever thought about killing somebody? And I don't mean when you're a little steamed and say, "I could just kill him (or her)," or whatever. What I'm asking here is if you've ever considered crossing that line for real.

No, of course, you haven't.

But I have. All the time. And I'm not the only one, either. All you have to do is watch TV or pick up a newspaper and see for yourself that there are lots of guys out there like me. Fed up. Pissed off.

My name is Eddie Becker, and I'm writing all this down to keep from going batshit crazy in this place. It might help. It might not. One thing's for sure though: bottling it up inside until I blow my top hasn't done me much good so far. So I sent away for some plain—I repeat, plain—notepads to write on. When they finally came and I saw the heading crawling across the top of the page, I almost ripped them to shreds. Someone at that company probably caught hell for that little screw-up, maybe even lost their job. Serves them right. Anyway, the notepads say "From the Desk of Edward Becker" in fancy gold writing. But I guess the joke's on me since my "desk" is nothing but a small tray that folds down from the cinderblock wall. I'm sitting at it now, the light from the corridor turning that squiggle at the top of the page into a gleaming, gold-toothed smirk. Outside my tiny barred window, the sky is still black as sin. Reminds me of that saying about it always being darkest just before the dawn.

It was Leon Conway, in here for butchering his wife with a claw hammer, who said I should write these thoughts down (actually, he used the word rants), though he didn't say it in a friendly way. I don't have any real friends to speak of. But friendly or not, I decided to take him up on it. They stuck me in here a year and a half ago, and I spend most of my time in this little concrete cracker box, so you can see how I might need a hobby or three to keep from banging my head against the wall until I bash my damn brains out.

I'm having a little trouble fixing on where to start. For one thing, I've never done this before—writing about myself, that is—so I'm not quite sure how to go about it. For another, that fucker Ramirez is awake and raising Cain a few cells down. "Momma! Momma!" he cries, over and over again, setting off a lively round of comebacks: "I got yo' momma right here," and, "Bitch can't talk just now, she got a mouthful." So I can barely hear myself think. Prison is bad (go figure), somewhere you sure as hell don't want to end up. The stuff that goes on in here . . . well, I don't really want to get into that and, besides, I'm sure you've already got a pretty good idea. What I want to talk about is how I ended up here in the first place. I guess I'll just bring you up to speed as best I can and then go on from there.

I was born on the night of December 8, 1980, in New York's Roosevelt Hospital. While my mother screamed on a blood-soaked gurney (or so I've been told) John Lennon was being pronounced dead somewhere under that very same roof. He went out and I came in. I think about that a lot.

We left New York when I was young, so I don't really remember that much about it. Mostly the noise, and buildings that seemed tall as mountains. When you're little it's like you're living in a world full of giants, all the time zigging and zagging to stay out from underfoot while they clump around you, rumbling like thunderclouds. I do remember being scared a lot, especially when my old man was riled or piss drunk, or both, which was most of the time.

Anyway, we wound up in Indiana, in a little flyspeck of a town called Lynnwood, and that's where I did most of my growing up. Grade school was tolerable, mostly because it got me out of the house, away from my mom's nagging (I don't think she ever forgave me for being born) and my dad's hard fists. I even managed to make what I thought was a pretty good friend, a guy named Steve Burdett. But everything changed during my freshman year at Truman High. What they did was bus a bunch of other kids in from the neighboring town of Edmund, and we all came together in the crumbling redbrick monstrosity just down the street from Lynnwood Grade School. So new blood was poured into the mix and, as was bound to happen, certain ones who had reigned in grade school somehow managed to slip to the bottom of the social ladder. I was one of those. I don't really know why, I guess I just got off on the wrong foot.

Right off the bat, this big clod named Travis Skinner decided he didn't like my face and made it his job to cause me misery on a daily basis—stuff like hiding my street clothes during gym, sticking signs on my back with witty statements like "Kick me," or "Will swaller for a dollar," and 'accidentally' tripping me in the hallway. On top of that, my measly circle of so-called friends from grade school more or less disowned me—even Steve Burdett. His betrayal hurt me more than I can put into words. Well . . . that's not really true. I know exactly how it felt. It felt like he squashed my heart in his hands like it was an overripe tomato.

At Truman, they taught all the usual junk, nothing of any real use to me as far as I could ever tell. But when Steve turned his back on me it was my first real lesson in high school—how cold-hearted the world really is, and how in the end we're all pretty much left for dead.

One day, after Phys Ed, while I was getting dressed in the locker room, I let it slip to Tommy Wannamaker that I was going to put a stop to Travis's pestering, though really I was only letting off steam. The last thing in the world I wanted to do was poke the bear. Anyway, news of my empty threat reached Travis in no time, so he was laying for me. When I tried to slip past him in the hallway he spun around in front of his open locker to face me down, a couple of books in the crook of his arm.

"Hey, punk," he said sociably, "I hear you're gonna kick my ass."

I kept my mouth shut.

Three or four kids heard Travis's comment and stopped to gawk at us. This caused a few others to gather around, damming the flow of students in the hallway like a log jam in a river. It reminds me of a line from some band in the '90s, I can't remember who: "Nothing attracts a crowd like a crowd."

"Whasamatter?" His voice was dripping with fake sympathy. "Your vagina hurt?"

I stayed mum.

Then Travis sneered at me, looking like an ape in a white T-shirt.

"You're dead," he growled.

I didn't mull it over, didn't give myself so much as a split second to think about it. I punched him in the nose as hard as I could. Blood gushed from his nostrils and his head snapped back like his neck was made of rubber. Thinking back on what happened next, it seems sort of funny to me now. But in that time, in that place, the last thing I wanted to do was laugh. Because things got very serious very fast, and I was scared out of my wits.

What happened was that Travis's head rocked back so hard it slammed inside his locker and got wedged there. His books tumbled forgotten to the floor at his feet while he twisted around like a fish on a hook, trying to pull his oversize melon out of that tight little space.

Then an uproar went through the crowd of kids surrounding us—catcalls, cheers, and shouts of "Fight! Fight!" They smelled blood. I stepped back and waited for Travis to free himself, a choice that right away brought me hisses and boos from the looky-loos.

I'm sure some—maybe most—of them couldn't understand why I didn't play the ace I'd been dealt. I mean, I had a clean shot if I wanted to take it. I don't think I understood it myself at the time. I'd like to say I backed off because I was being all noble and obeying that unwritten law not to kick a man when he's down. But that would be a lie. I think the real reason I waited there with my knees knocking and my heart thumping was that I had something to prove, to myself and everyone else there. When this was over, good or bad, there would be no arguing over the outcome. So I stood there feeling clammy and half sick, because I had poked the bear after all, and now it was too late to turn back.

Travis frantically yanked his head from inside the locker, damn near ripping his ears off in the process. Blood was flowing freely down his chin and neck. A red rose bloomed at the top of his white T-shirt. His face was flushed and his eyes were brimming with tears—partly because of the pain, I'm sure, but mostly I think from shame. At first, he just stood there huffing and puffing like a mad bull, glaring at me with a mix of wonder and pure hate. I tell you if looks could kill I would have been knocked dead as a turd right then and there on that ugly green tile floor.

He charged.

And that's when a weird thing happened.

All at once it was like time stretched out, and I was watching Travis slog forward in slow motion. When he drifted close enough, his huge hammy fists swept toward me in one sluggish, easy-to-clock roundhouse after another—about as hard to dodge as a steam engine chugging toward you from around a distant bend. The crowd of kids swayed and wafted around us like seaweed. Frail old Mrs. Grumman, our English teacher, floated down the hallway in our direction. On the wall, the clock's second hand hung frozen. It was all very unreal. Years later I watched a show about nature on the Discovery Channel and saw how flies see the world. To them, we're like these big creeping mountains, even when we think we're moving fast. That's why it's so hard to catch a fly. They always see you coming. It was the same with me that day.

Travis never laid a finger on me. I danced around him easily and, while the crowd egged me on, beat him unrecognizable.

No one bothered me again after that.

That was my second real lesson in high school: that violence, whatever you might think of it, is sometimes the only way out.

So what the hell does all this have to do with why I'm in the joint? Well, I'll tell you. I changed, or was changed, just as surely as the sky outside my window, which is now a deep smoldering red ember.

Like I said before, my old man was pretty hateful and I guess the acorn didn't fall far from the tree. I think giving Travis his comeuppance was what set off the same thing in me, though I'm sure it would have happened sooner or later, no matter what. Anyway, I started getting pissed all the time over every little thing. I couldn't help it, it just seemed like there was so much to get pissed about. But here's the thing: whenever I was in this mood, everything around me would slow down the way it did that day with Travis and all of a sudden I was like that fly again. It was a trip, kind of an out-of-body thing, like déjàvu.

After I graduated high school I mostly bummed around for a couple of years. I had so many different jobs, I lost count. I did everything from political fundraising to hauling garbage—both pretty much the same when you think about it. But nothing ever seemed to fit, or I didn't.

Finally I up and came to California, thinking a change of scenery might do me good. I got a job in a paper factory that was suffocating in the summer and freezing in the winter. Don't ever let anybody tell you it doesn't get cold out here, because it does. Anyway, my boss and my coworkers didn't like me much (I've never been what you'd call a team player) and the feeling was mutual. Every day I spent inside that place just pushed me closer to the edge.

The outside world wasn't much better, either. The establishment, the system, whatever you want to call it, really started getting under my skin. Too many stupid rules. After a while, it got so I would get aggravated just seeing some guy in a suit and tie, and I couldn't watch TV without wanting to slam my foot through it. More and more often, the world kept slowing down.

I felt like I was running on a wheel, one that got me nowhere, just helped to power this gigantic machine moving around me. But that's the way it is. They want your heart and soul, your blood and balls, and they use you up until there's nothing left but a pile of bones bleaching in the sun.

Crazy talk, huh? Well, I'll tell you, it's easy just to call someone crazy and have done with it. But it seems to me that nobody ever wonders what made them crazy in the first place. I admit some people are just plain off their nut, like the lady who said God told her to drown her kids in the bathtub like a couple of stray kittens. Or the guy who thinks aliens are sending him messages through his radio. But then there are those average, everyday people who just come to a point in their lives when they've had enough.

I remember seeing on the news that some guy walked into a DMV office somewhere in the Midwest and opened fire with an assault rifle, killing some of the workers there. Everyone always acts so surprised when things like that happen. But I'm never surprised. Things being the way they are, some people just get tired of being pushed around. They finally step down off that hamster wheel and file a grievance that can't be ignored. So no, I'm not a bit surprised by such things. I'm only surprised they don't happen more often.

I'm not simply, or even mostly, talking about the usual fuckery going on out there: crooked politicians, the rich getting richer while the poor just keep getting the shaft, and the working class being broken like a rented mule. That stuff's easy to see. No, I'm talking about a slow-moving rottenness, one that's creeping into the world like cancer. You have to be a fly to see that.

And I see people. They talk at, not with, one another. I was getting a cup of joe at Starbucks one day, and from the counter I noticed four teenage girls sitting at a nearby table. They were as still as stones, their heads bowed, their hands in their laps like they were praying or something. Then I saw the cell phones in their hands, their thumbs flying over the keys in a mad blur. All at once one of them looked up and squealed at the girl sitting across from her, "I know, right?"

Technology is a great thing, or at least it can be, I guess. But I can see it slowly sapping people of their humanity. I heard or read somewhere that even though the world has practically been changed into one gigantic neighborhood by technology, individuals are more alone than they ever were before. Too bad for them. As for me, I don't think I ever had much humanity in me to start with. Being bred in garbage, living in it, shitting in it, eating it, how could I be anything other than a fucking fly?

Some find relief in religion. I never could. I remember some people at the paper factory were all wound up one day about the upcoming Easter holiday and the plans they had with their families. I couldn't help myself. I jumped in the conversation, asking all innocent-like where the Easter bunny showed up in the Bible. I guess I don't have to tell you this rubbed a few of them the wrong way, and I got called to the human resources department, where they gave me a crash course on the subject of zero tolerance in the workplace. And, of course, my little comment got me the cold shoulder from everybody for a while. Not that I cared. I'd rather not be bothered than listen to people who feel like they have to fill in the blanks with a lot of pointless small talk.

I spent much of my time at work just staring out the window at the sky (I still do that, only now my view is spoiled by bars). When I was a kid in Indiana I'd stretch out on our picnic table in the backyard and watch the cottony clouds float by for hours, picturing faces and elephants and sailboats. And on clear nights I stared at the stars sprinkled across the heavens and felt very small and unimportant. Feeling small and unimportant can be a comfort.

Why do we lose that curiosity, that feeling of wonder, when we grow up? Is it because we're too busy running on that wheel? When we're at work we watch the clock, waiting for the mind-numbing dullness to end so we can escape our chains for a spell. We plan our days, our weeks, even our years in advance, trying to outwit time. But it's funny because we end up spending most of that time wishing it away. John Lennon said it best: Life is what happens to you while you're busy making other plans.

When he was taken out and I was brought in, I feel like the scales were tipped out of balance, you know? It was like the world got cheated in more ways than one. Because the world got me, and it was not an even trade. Not by a long shot.

They say I'm a danger to society—a fly in the ointment, you might say. I can't argue with that. No matter how you slice it, I'm the bad guy in this story, the loser with the big chip on his shoulder, and I was bound to take it out on somebody sooner or later.

Which brings me to the reason they locked me up.

It was a hot Tuesday night and I was standing in line at the 7-Eleven with a six-pack of Corona in my hand. The only other customer in the store was the guy ahead of me, this slick-looking dude in a dark blue suit, his black hair perfectly mussed. His stubby, hairy-knuckled fingers were decked out with flashy rings that winked in the light, and he'd splashed on so much catch-me-fuck-me cologne that it burned my nostrils. He was buying a bunch of lottery scratch-off tickets and asking the clerk, this young Asian woman, different questions about each and every goddamn one of them. At the same time, the two of them were going on and on about whatever the hell popped into their heads, totally ignoring me standing there with a six-pack of beer that wasn't getting any colder. After a while, I cleared my throat to get their attention. The guy glanced over his shoulder at me with heavy-lidded eyes. He looked me up and down like I was smeared with shit or something, then turned away again. I would have let it go at that, but I heard him mutter under his breath, "Fucking asswipe." Then he went right on with his little confab with the clerk, forgetting me completely. And mistakenly.

The world slowed to a crawl.

I looked down at the cold bottles of beer in my hand, beads of sweat starting to trickle down their necks, and my fingers tightened around the carton's handle. Keeping my feet firmly planted, I twisted to the right at my waist and held the Coronas out behind me. I hefted them a couple of times, testing their weight. I thought they would do. The clerk gave me an uninterested glance and yammered on without missing a beat. Probably thought I was just stretching my back. I took one last look around to make sure that the three of us still had the place to ourselves. Then I swung the six-pack at the dude's head, giving it everything I had. I watched it explode against his temple in a sparkling, slow-motion shower.

It seemed like I had time to think a thousand thoughts while he drifted toward the floor, his scattered lottery tickets hanging in midair all around him in shiny flashes of red, blue and green. But all I remember is being stupidly fascinated by an untouched strip of black stubble running along the underside of his otherwise clean-shaven jawline. It was like every mystery in the universe was there, focused down to that one spot, and I was hypnotized. The moment spun out for years, for ages, forever. At last, he came to rest at my feet with a soft thud. His eyelids fluttered as he lay there bleeding from the wallop I'd just given him, and I could see tiny shards of glass twinkling in his black lashes. Lottery tickets were strewn across the floor from here till Sunday. There was a muffled, underwater sound droning on in my ears—the clerk screaming.

Standing there over the guy, I felt like I was having one of those dreams where you know exactly how it's going to play out. I dropped to one knee in the widening puddle of beer and blood, feeling its wetness seep through my jeans. All of the bottles were smashed to smithereens, but one. It lay at the foot of the potato chip rack like a wounded soldier, still mostly okay except for its shattered bottom. The fluorescent lights bounced brightly off its sides. I reached over and picked it up by the neck, pointing the sharp end away from me. The guy's eyelids had flown open and he stared uncomprehendingly up at me. Cutting through the mixed tang of blood and beer was the smell of his shitty cologne, and my anger turned white hot. I grabbed a handful of his hair and tilted his head back, exposing that bristly patch his Gillette had missed.

"Let me get that for you," I remember saying, then I stuck him like a pig and watched him bleed out, his eyes dimming like a couple of burnt-out light bulbs.

So they put me in this cell, and that, as they say, is that.

Am I sorry about what happened? Of course I am. But it doesn't matter anymore. Truth is, I'm not sure if anything ever mattered to begin with.

They say life's a journey, not a destination. Tell me something I don't know. I've never gotten anywhere in my whole stupid life. And it seems like the trip has mostly been uphill.

Oh, woe is me, right? Well, I'm not making excuses for what I did, or what I am. What's done is done. I only wanted to tell the story. Take from it what you will. Just one piece of advice: Next time some guy cuts you off in traffic, think twice about flipping him off. Because that guy could be someone like me.

Well, there it is. I don't know if putting all this down helped or not, but either way, that's all I have to say. One good thing: down the hall, Ramirez has finally simmered down. It'll be breakfast call soon. I guess I could eat. Sunlight is starting to spill over the horizon, turning the sky a bruised pinkish purple. And dig this.

There's a fly buzzing outside my window.

THE PRESENT

November 4, 1965

His fists rained down again and again, until she barely had strength left to ward off the blows. Mary prayed to a god she'd long since stopped believing in that Rachel wouldn't come home from school just yet. Above the sink, the kitchen clock, an ugly yellow monstrosity shaped like a duck (a gift from Ted's mother), said 3:05 PM. That was about the time Rachel usually breezed through the kitchen door. Unless she decided to stop off at her best friend Amy's house. Occasionally she did.

"How many times have I told you to have supper on the goddamn table when I get home from work, *woman?*" Ted punctuated his question with a right cross, this one landing on the side of Mary's neck. It set her whole face on fire.

It wasn't as if Rachel never witnessed these beatings. She'd seen plenty. Still, it didn't prevent Mary from wanting to shield her daughter as much as possible from the horrors that took place in the

Garver household, a place that Mary had come to think of as her prison.

Ted wouldn't allow Mary to work. This was partly because Ted's father, Hank (a real son of a bitch if there ever was one), believed that a woman's place was in the home, and Ted was a chip off the proverbial block. But the main reason Mary was forbidden to get a job was that Ted didn't want her turning up in public with fresh bruises every couple of weeks. Yet he knew that she couldn't very well live her entire life inside the house. So he was careful to administer his punishments below the neck when he could. Only sometimes, he got carried away.

Like now.

"You don't appreciate how hard I work for this family"—Ted brought his fist down like a hammer on the top of Mary's head—"but by God, you *will*." He gathered a handful of her hair and began dragging her across the floor toward the stove. That last blow had felt like it almost broke her neck, and Mary cried out as fire rushed down her spine. Her yellow cotton dress rode up above her knees, which scudded painfully across the linoleum.

When they reached the stove Ted flipped on the burner. Mary realized what he intended and she screamed and thrashed wildly. Ted seized her right wrist in his left hand, then drove an elbow into her forehead. Motes exploded before Mary's eyes, expanding like a galaxy of tiny dying suns until there was nothing left but a thick gray haze blanketing her vision. She felt herself slipping away, all cares and concerns scattering, and she welcomed oblivion.

The flame brought her back, though. Mary shrieked. She bucked and flailed and tried desperately to jerk her hand away from the burner. But Ted was much stronger, and he held her fast, letting the bright blue flame lick the back of her hand.

He didn't hold it there for long, but it felt to Mary like an eternity. When he let her go she crumpled to the floor and cradled her blackened hand to her chest, hot tears streaming down her cheeks.

Ted gave an exasperated sigh. "Go to the bathroom and clean yourself up," he said as if admonishing a child.

Mary lay there a little longer. Not too long, though. It wouldn't do to ignore her husband's wishes. At last, she rose and, still favoring her hand, moved like a ghost from the kitchen, down the hallway, and into the bathroom.

"And don't think this gets you out of fixing supper," Ted called after her.

Mary had tried to tell him why his supper was late—that the bus she usually caught to the grocery store had broken down, so the company had to send another one out—but it was no use. There were no excuses in Ted Garver's world.

Half an hour later, Mary was at the stove frying pork chops when Rachel walked in. The girl's smile collapsed when she saw her mother's bruised face and bandaged hand, and a small whimper escaped her lips. Mary cast an anxious glance down the hallway toward the living room where a football game blared on the TV, then turned back to her daughter. Mary shook her head slightly while meeting Rachel's gaze. *Don't say anything,* that look said. *It'll just set him off again.* Then she offered Rachel a hopeful smile and a nod, which said, *I'll be okay, don't worry.* Tears welled up in Rachel's eyes. She pressed the heels of her hands to her eyes, her chest hitching once, quietly. Her head bobbed as she swallowed the huge lump in her throat. Then she rubbed away the tears and wiped them on the front of her dress. The sad smile she returned to her mother broke Mary's heart. It was a heart that had been broken so many times it was a wonder it was still beating.

That night, in the darkness of their bedroom, Ted asked, "How's your hand?" Mary jumped. She thought he had been asleep.

"Not bad," she lied. It felt like fire ants were devouring her flesh. But Mary knew better than to complain too much. "I took some aspirin."

He was silent for so long that she thought he finally *had* fallen asleep. Then he spoke again. "You know I don't like hurting you."

"I know."

"Do you really?"

"Yes."

A pause. "I just get a little mad sometimes, that's all. Doesn't mean I don't love you."

"I know."

A longer pause. "Do you still love me?"

Here it comes, Mary thought. "Of course."

Ted heaved a deep sigh. "I'm glad," he said. "I don't like thinking about things like that, like you not loving me anymore, or you trying to leave me and taking Rachel away from me."

"That won't ever happen," Mary said.

"But if it *did* happen," he said, "I just don't know what I'd do."

Mary waited.

"Probably something really bad," Ted said.

November 13, 1965

Saturday. Mary was making breakfast when Rachel cried out in the bathroom. Without thinking, Mary flipped the burner off and rushed down the hallway. She flung open the door. And there stood Rachel, still dripping wet from the bath, a towel held loosely against her body with one hand, her other hand held out in front of her, trembling and slick with blood. Mary's eyes were drawn to the other redness between her daughter's thin white thighs, and her first thought was, *Oh, God, I never talked with her about this.*

Rachel looked up with tear-filled eyes. "What's happening, Mama?"

At that moment, Ted appeared at Mary's back. "You okay, girl? You cut yourself?"

Mary turned and caught Ted's gaze...saw his expression slowly change, his face become wooden. "Oh," he said.

Mary returned her attention to Rachel, who had lifted the towel higher in a self-conscious effort to cover more of herself. Ted made a disgusted sound. "Take care of this," he growled, pushing Mary forward. He stomped away down the hall, cursing under his breath. Something about "another goddamn woman in the house."

Mary shut the bathroom door behind her.

November 28, 1965

"What the goddamn hell!" Ted's voice boomed from the bathroom. Both Mary and Rachel jumped, Rachel spilling some of her popcorn from its Tupperware bowl. They'd been sitting on the sofa watching the Ed Sullivan Show on television. Now they looked up as Ted stormed into the room holding a tube of red lipstick in his fist. He held it out before them.

"What is this?" he demanded.

Rachel's eyes went wide.

Mary opened her mouth to claim the lipstick belonged to her, even though she was perfectly aware of the consequences. Back when they were dating, she had worn makeup, and Ted never complained. Indeed, he seemed to like it. After she became pregnant with Rachel, however, his attitude began to change. He made snide remarks about her looks and her fragrance. Once they were married, he forbade her to use such things anymore, said she had no business tempting men, since she had already snagged one. And in his mind, that was what it all came down to, really. She had caught him with her feminine wiles just as surely as a hunter's prey is ensnared by the scent of bait. And when she went and "got herself" knocked up, he was truly and hopelessly had.

But Mary never got the words out, because Rachel volunteered, "I just wanted to try it, Daddy. Just to see what it looked like."

Ted hurled the tube across the room, where it struck the wall, leaving a bright red smudge before clattering to the floor.

He turned on Rachel.

"You little whore."

Ted unbuckled his belt and drew the leather through the loops like he was unsheathing a sword.

Rachel bolted off the couch, popcorn exploding everywhere. She tried to run, but the living room was too small and Ted was too fast. He seized her by her wrist. Rachel cried out. Mary was up instantly, mindlessly charging to her daughter's defense. She lashed out, clawing at Ted's face, the first time she had ever retaliated against him. But again, Ted was too quick. He dodged the swipe of her hooked fingers by feinting back, then drove a battering ram of a fist into her right eye. Mary went down hard on her back, the world going gray around the edges, the light fading.

The last thing she heard was the sound of Ted's belt against Rachel's flesh (*thwack, thwack, thwack,* over and over again) and Rachel screaming, "No, Daddy, no no *nooooooooooo!*"

Then blackness.

December 3, 1965

Mary wandered along John F. Kennedy Drive, tugging her coat collar tight against the bitter cold and giving the store windows only desultory glances. Although the afternoon was gray and misty, she wore her big tortoise-shell sunglasses.

The street's Christmas decorations gleamed and twinkled in stark and colorful contrast to the gloomy backdrop of the day. People bustled to and fro, bright packages in their mittened hands, and Mary knew that the crowds would only get thicker, the streets and stores busier, between now and the big day. She looked at the people passing by, at their seemingly happy faces, and felt utterly alone.

Mary knew she should be home doing Friday's chores—Ted liked the house to be spick and span come the weekend—but the walls had started closing in on her, and she thought if she didn't get out for a while she would simply suffocate. So she'd thrown on her coat and dashed out the door, turning a deaf ear to the frightened voice in the back of her mind: *Ted won't like coming home to a dirty house, you know. Won't like it at all.* He'd most likely get upset and... well, she knew what would happen then, didn't she? But that didn't stop her.

Because she was used to it by now. At least, that's what she tried to tell herself. Used to the pain. The fear. Deep down, she knew that wasn't true, of course. The real truth was that, sometimes, even fear was not enough to hold back the need to feel *free,* if only for a little while.

She started to feel dizzy, experienced a light, fluttering sensation in the pit of her stomach, like when you floated over a hill in a fast-moving car or plunged headlong toward the earth on a roller coaster. She braced her hand against the wall of a nearby building for support, her head spinning unpleasantly. When a man paused on the sidewalk and inquired in a far-away voice whether she was all right, Mary thought she answered yes, though she couldn't be sure.

She waited, nauseated, for the vertigo to ebb. It seemed interminable. Finally, she gathered herself, took a deep breath, squared her shoulders, and resumed her trek down JFK Drive. Or what she had thought was JFK. But when Mary reached the intersection, she saw that she stood on the corner of Keeling Street and Fourth Avenue. She was confused. Fourth Avenue was right where it should be, but how had she gotten off of JFK Drive without being aware of it? Not only that, but she knew this part of town like the back of her hand, and she had never even *heard* of Keeling Street.

She stopped a young woman passing by with a toddler in tow.

"Excuse me. Isn't this John F. Kennedy Drive?"

The woman looked at Mary as if she thought she might be joking. Then she asked it out loud. "Are you kidding?"

"Um. No."

"Don't they usually wait until someone's dead before they name a street after them?" the woman asked. The toddler, a little boy, goggled up at Mary.

Mary stared at her. What in the world was this woman talking about?

The woman's expression went from amused to puzzled, then turned to concern. She searched Mary's face intently, tried to scan the eyes behind the dark sunglasses, and Mary felt her face flush despite the cold.

"Are you okay, honey?" the woman asked.

"Unee," the boy echoed.

"I'm fine," Mary muttered absently. "Thank you." She turned and stepped off the curb, and jumped at the sound of a blaring horn and screeching tires. She gaped at the wide-eyed man behind the wheel, her legs turning to water. The smell of burnt rubber filled her nostrils. The driver leaned out his window.

"Jeez Louise, lady! Watch where you're goin' why dont'cha!"

Mary stepped back up onto the curb and pressed her palm to her heaving chest in an effort to keep her heart from tearing itself loose and jumping out onto the sidewalk. She tried to say she was sorry to the irate man, but her lips couldn't form the words. He rolled on through the intersection, shaking his head. It was then that she noticed the make and model of the car. It was a white Ford Galaxie 500. She should know: Ted drove the exact same one. Except there on the front quarter panel, where the chrome Galaxie 500 logo should be attached, it said Impel.

Ford Impel?

"Miss, are you sure you're okay?"

Mary turned and saw the woman with the toddler staring at her. The boy's mouth formed an O. Mary nodded, looked both ways on Fourth Avenue, then crossed and continued along Keeling Street.

Mary had read the phrase *her mind reeled* before but had never fully grasped it until now. As she walked along a street that should by all rights have been named after their slain president, Mary began searching for other incongruities. It didn't take long to spot one. In the window of a record shop, an album cover leaned against a portable record player. It showed the rock group, the Beatles, whose music Rachel was absolutely crazy about. Mary enjoyed their music too, though she would never admit it to Ted, a devout George Jones fan. She thought their songs were catchy and clever. She'd become familiar with their faces from the posters in Rachel's room, and had heard her daughter coo their names enough times, though the only one she could ever remember was Ringo.

The cover in the window was of the band's new album, *Rubber Soul*, released that very day. The Fab Four stared at the camera, the album title appearing above their heads in fat orange letters. Except Ringo was missing. In his place stood a young man Mary had never seen before, his hairstyle unlike his bandmates' "mop tops." It looked more like Elvis's Pompadour. Their first names had been dashed off next to their faces. His simply said, Pete.

Mary frowned at the cover for a long time.

Farther down the street she froze in front of a store called Dave's Fine Appliances. In the window were a trio of televisions displayed at different levels. All three were tuned to the same station, which showed footage of a man in a spacesuit hopping around on some dusty, desolate surface. A small tinny-sounding speaker was connected to the upper corner of the store's doorjamb so that passersby could hear, as well as watch, whatever was happening on those screens. Accompanying the footage of the spaceman was the familiar voice of Walter Cronkite:

"And here we see astronaut John Herman, the first man ever to walk on the surface of the moon. These images were captured only minutes after Scorpio Seven's historic landing four days ago, November twenty-ninth, Nineteen Sixty-five."

The scene switched to Cronkite himself, seated behind his desk. He was pinching the bridge of his nose, presumably wiping tears from the corners of his eyes. *"I never get tired of watching that,"* he said.

Mary was stunned.

She whirled around to share her excitement with someone, *anyone.*

But, of course, these people already knew.

We landed on the moon, she thought, astonished. *In this place, anyway. Wherever this place is.*

Her eyes were drawn to a man across the street. He was leaning in the open doorway of a building with the uninspiring name PAWN

SHOP over the entrance. He was tall, thin, with skin so pale and hair so white/blond that he might have been an albino. He leaned in the doorway with his arms crossed, dressed in ragged blue jeans and a black t-shirt with the word NIRVANA across the chest in bold white letters. The man was completely out of place. Like a clown at a cocktail party. Yet no one else appeared to notice him at all.

He looked straight at her. The corners of his thin lips curled up in a smile, and his hand rose like the head of a cobra from a wicker basket. With a slim index finger, he motioned for her to approach him.

She did, feeling almost as if she were floating across Keeling Street. When she stood before him, he said, "Hi, sweetness."

His irises were so pale blue they looked like ice chips, and something indefinable moved (*writhed?*) behind them, stirring within Mary several different emotions at once. One of those stirrings found its insidious way between her legs, and Mary was mortified. Even more so when he gave her a knowing smile. Her face burned, and the fire spread down her neck to her torso.

"You looking for something?" His voice was like silk.

"I…that is…" Mary felt the same way she had as a schoolgirl, tongue-tied with one of the cute boys or popular girls. But she was a grown woman, for heaven's sake. And this man wasn't even all that attractive. Odd, yes, but certainly not handsome. Still, she couldn't deny he possessed a kind of…quality. A strange magnetism. She felt that tickle down there again and thought her face would burst into flames at any moment.

"A Christmas gift for the hubby, perhaps?"

Mary gasped and realized she had not been breathing. She exhaled the word, "Yes," in a relieved rush of air.

"I think I have just the thing." He gave her a sly, conspiratorial wink. "C'mon inside."

He turned and disappeared into the store. Mary followed or at least started to. She halted just past the threshold, her eyes unable to penetrate the dimness of the interior.

"You're gonna have to take those shades off, you wanna see," he called from deeper inside the room.

Mary hesitated.

"It's okay," he said. "No judgment here."

How does he know? she wondered, her heart speeding up.

"I'm psychic," he said as if indeed reading her mind.

Mary stayed where she was. She heard boots scuffing against a wooden floor as he moved across the room.

"Actually," he said, "I'm just not stupid. A woman sporting dark sunglasses on a day like today usually means, one) she's blind, which you ain't, two) she's got one humdinger of a hangover, which *could* be the case, but my spidey sense tells me otherwise, or three) somebody's been tuning up on her face. Number three's my guess."

Mary reached up and dragged the glasses off her face, revealing what she knew was an unlovely black and purple bruise around her right eye.

"Well now," the man said, and Mary heard a tightness in his voice, "give the man a cigar."

He stood behind a long counter in a room shaped like a boxcar. A dusty hardwood floor stretched away toward the rear. The place appeared to be cram-packed with every kind of knick-knack and gewgaw imaginable: antique lamps; clocks (one, a black and white cat whose golf ball eyes swiveled disturbingly back and forth, counting off the seconds); cheap artwork; record players and radios; guitars; various containers; watches and jewelry and pistols (behind a glass case under the counter), and a million sundry other items. On the wall behind the counter, like a formation of soldiers, stood a row of long guns.

"Step right up, little lady," the pale man invited.

Mary approached the counter.

He bent down and appeared to reach into a section under the counter where a sign that read WE BUY AND SELL leaned against the inside of the glass, obstructing her view. In that moment something told her she should leave. Right then. Get out and retrace her steps back along Keeling Street until it somehow, impossibly, became JFK Drive again. Get to the bus stop. Go home. And try to forget this upside down day ever happened.

Then something else told her no. She had to stay, *must* stay. It was that same feeling from before, the one that recognized her need to feel free, if only for a while. She didn't know why this should be, but then she didn't understand *anything* anymore.

The man stood up, and on the countertop, he placed a simple wooden container the size and shape of a cigar box.

"I think this little item is just what ol' hubby needs," he said, smiling.

Mary looked curiously at the box.

"Yes," the man said, "I do believe it's just what he deserves."

Now the man's expression turned sober. His mouth formed a grim line.

"Now, whatever you do, Mary," he said, "don't touch it."

"How do you know…" Mary's voice trailed off because the pale man had opened the box.

And what was inside was the most terrible thing she had ever seen.

December 25, 1965

Mary set the stack of pancakes down on the kitchen table, then settled herself gingerly onto her chair. Her rear end still stung from Ted's belt. He'd taken her over his knee the night before because, according to him, Mary had "sassed" him when he came home from Mickey's Bar, spoiling his Christmas cheer. In truth, all she had done was ask him to take his slushy boots off at the front door so he wouldn't track the mess inside. It was Friday evening, after all, and she had waxed the floor that day and cleaned the house within an inch of its life. Mary had made sure to do this every Friday since that particular Friday she visited the pawn shop with the mysterious pale man. Because that day she never got around to cleaning up, and Ted punished her severely for her laziness.

When Mary left the pawn shop that day, the wooden box poking from the top of her purse, she stepped out onto John F. Kennedy Drive. Across the street, Dave's Fine Appliances was once again the Soap-N-Suds Laundromat. And when she turned around, she wasn't at all surprised to see no pawn shop there. The entire building, in fact, was just…gone. In its place stood an empty lot. She went directly home and did what the pale man had told her to do.

Then she waited.

In a sudden motion, Ted reached across the table for the bottle of syrup. Rachel, who sat across from Mary, flinched. She did that a lot these days. Mary ate her breakfast silently, each bite slow and deliberate. It was the longest meal of her life.

But finally it was over, and following their tradition, carried over from Ted's childhood, they all repaired to the living room to gather around the fake tree, drink eggnog, and open their gifts, each in turn. Rachel was first. She received a pair of plaid skirts with complimentary tops, the Beatles' new *Rubber Soul* album (this one with Ringo's face on the cover), and a new record player to spin it on. Rachel squealed with delight over the record and hugged both her parents. But Mary couldn't help noticing Rachel's lip curl in distaste while embracing her dad.

Next, it was Mary's turn. She got a new iron, a Toastmaster toaster—"Maybe now you'll quit burning it," Ted told her—and some pots and pans.

"Last but not least," Mary said, reaching under the tree and retrieving a package wrapped in shiny red paper and topped with a green bow. Ted sat on the sofa, glassy-eyed from the splash of rum he'd added to his eggnog. She placed the present on the coffee table in front of her husband. It was about the size of a cigar box.

Ted gave her a look that contained one part appreciation and two parts warning. "You better not have spent too much on this."

"No, Ted." In truth, she hadn't paid a dime.

Ted's eyes gazed into hers with dark promise for another few seconds. Then he grinned.

"Well, all right then," Ted said and began unwrapping his gift. While he was thus occupied, Mary looked from where she was seated on the floor up at Rachel, who sat on the footstool, her new album on her lap. Rachel looked back at her.

Mary gazed intently at Rachel for a long moment, turned her eyes away and fixed them on Ted's present, then looked back at her daughter once more. Mary gave a slight nod.

Realization dawned in Rachel's eyes. Her mouth became a grim line. She nodded back.

She understood. Maybe not everything. But enough.

"What have we here?" Ted said. Before him sat a simple wooden box.

"Merry Christmas, Ted," said Mary.

Ted opened the box.

"Wha—?"

Mary saw darkness gathering around the box. Heard a rush of air. She flinched when it exploded into splinters as the thing inside it expanded. It was a perfect black circle. A hole. And the light of day in its immediate vicinity was being sucked into it.

So was Ted.

He tried to rise, to tear himself away. But the hole was far too powerful. Far too hungry.

Like a mouth, Mary thought.

She stood up to get a better look, and from the corner of her eye saw that Rachel was also getting to her feet. They watched.

The noise of air rushing into opening was deafening, like a jet engine, and Mary felt her ears pop.

Ted screamed, but even the sound of that was being sucked down the hole. He braced his hands against the top of the coffee table on either side of the aperture, every muscle in his body straining in an effort to prevent being sucked in like a spider through a vacuum cleaner tube.

When Rachel started to take a step forward, Mary shouted at her to stop. She remembered the pale man saying not to get too close once the box was opened, that the hole was unbiased. Which was why he exhorted her to wrap the box the minute she arrived home with it, and by no means to open it.

The pall of darkness expanded around the hole as Ted battled for his life.

"Mary...please. Help me!" he shrieked, but the words were torn from his lips and swept away. Mary now fought to draw a breath. It was as if she were trying to suck the air into her lungs through a straw. She glanced over and saw that Rachel struggled as well. Her chest was heaving up and down.

The hole widened again, and Ted's left hand plunged inside. He tumbled into the darkness, but at the last second his right hand caught on the rim. He reached out and clawed at the coffee table, seized its edge. Mary didn't understand how the table could still be standing there, intact, despite being almost completely breached by the hole. It hurt her mind to look at it.

It was getting harder and harder to breathe, and the scream of rushing air was pressing painfully against her eardrums.

She looked at Rachel. "We've got to get out of here!" she yelled. "If we don't we're going to suffocate—"

"Mom, look!" Rachel pointed at the hole.

Mary looked. And saw another hand, mottled and gray, reaching out of the hole to grasp Ted's hand. It was twice a large as Ted's hand, however, and its fingers—all six of them—were tipped with sharp black claws. It enclosed Ted's hand, and then dragged it out of sight.

The hole began to shrink. It looked like a puddle of oil receding into sand. As it dwindled, the noise of surging air died with it, and that area of the room gradually brightened.

The hole disappeared with a *pop* and a belch of the foulest stench Mary had ever smelled before. She wanted to retch. Rachel, too, was wrinkling her nose. But after a short time, the odor was gone as well.

Mary took a deep breath, looked at her daughter, and smiled.

Rachel returned it.

Mary knew they'd have much to talk about over the coming days and weeks. Much to do.

But there would be time.

And maybe in time, even the pain would be gone.

UGLY

If I'd been driving to work that day I never would have seen it happen, but my car was in the shop. So there I sat in the very back of a crowded San Diego city bus heading down Mira Mesa Boulevard and watching two assholes rag on some poor girl.

"What a cow," said the kid in the Chargers jersey.

"Moo," his buddy added. The Chargers fan was a whip-thin white guy with a mop of blond hair. His friend was big and black and wore a Lakers jersey. Couple of real sports.

They sat halfway down on the long bench seat, directly across from her, speaking in low tones, but not really trying too hard to be discreet. She knew they were talking about her, but acted used to it. I guess she probably was. Still, I saw the hurt in her eyes at their remarks. But all the while she kept a smile pasted on that homely face of hers.

Her name was Alice Unger and she always caught the bus to her waitress job at Denny's. I learned this from her conversation with the older Asian woman sitting beside her. The woman smiled and nodded as Alice went on and on, and I doubted she understood much English. Alice seemed oblivious, though, happy just to be talking.

"I wouldn't fuck that with your dick," said the blond.

"I appreciate that," his partner replied.

They both cracked up.

I looked at Alice. She was probably twenty-five but looked easily two decades older. She slumped like a lumpy sack of potatoes in her brown uniform. Her face was ablaze with acne and her nose was bulbous and red as a Christmas ornament. Her loose hair, a shade lighter than her outfit, bristled like a scarecrow's.

"I really like working at Denny's," she prattled on to her captive audience. Her tongue seemed too large for her mouth, which caused her to speak with a slight lisp. "I like the customers."

The white kid nudged his pal and muttered, "How the hell they s'posed to eat with a face like that hanging over 'em?"

His buddy shook his head in commiseration.

Seated catercorner to me, an old man leaned forward and spoke up. "Why don't you two shut your holes?"

The big black dude fixed him with a dangerous gaze and said, "Why don't you come up here and shut 'em for us?"

His mouth a grim line, the old man leaned back on the bench, leaving me in the black kid's line of sight. His eyes offered a challenge. I dropped my own toward the floor, told myself I had no skin in this game. I wasn't the only one. Everyone else stared out the windows or buried their noses in a book or smartphone. I felt sweat trickle down my sides. When the punk lost interest in me I chanced a look up into the big rearview mirror at the front of the bus and saw the driver's scanning eyes. They slid past mine and moved on.

Finally, we came to Alice's stop. She said goodbye to the Asian woman, who smiled and nodded. Alice teetered down the aisle toward the exit. From where I sat I could see a prominent hump high up on her back. It made me think of that old movie with Charles Laughton. I think those of us who remained on the bus breathed a collective sigh of relief at her departure. I could swear I felt the air get lighter.

The two assholes followed her off the bus.

Those who stayed on board watched Alice start off along Mira Mesa, some even moving from the other side of the bus to peer at her through the windows.

The white dude began to lurch along behind her, mocking her, swinging from side to side with his arms in the air, like an ape. His friend guffawed, stepped backward onto the curb, lost his balance, and stumbled in front of the bus and out of sight.

We heard the screech of rubber on pavement, then a loud thump followed by a sickening thwack sound, like raw meat being slapped down on a butcher's block.

We all flew as one to the left side of the bus as if it had suddenly been flipped onto its side. Clambering from a white BMW was a man in a shirt and tie, a forgotten cellphone in his hand. The Beemer's hood looked like it had been punched by a giant fist. A few yards beyond the car lay the black kid on his back, blood rapidly pooling around his head. The man in the shirt and tie took two or three shaky steps forward, did a little weaving dance, then bent over and threw up on his expensive shoes.

The other kid ran into the street and fell to his knees beside his friend. "Russell!" he screamed. The cars on our side of the median were stopped dead. On the other side, they crawled by, the people inside gaping at the grisly scene.

Alice appeared. She knelt down beside the kid's body and pressed her fingertips to his still chest.

And that's when it happened.

Alice's face began to get uglier if that was possible. Her nose swelled to nearly twice its size. Her face erupted in even more acne, splitting and bleeding in places. Her hair frizzed up as if she'd seized a live wire, and the breeze carried tufts of it away. On her back, the hump began to rise like a shifting land mass. It split her uniform blouse straight down the middle and popped her plain white bra. She threw her head back and cried out, her thick tongue protruding from her mouth.

"No more, *pleeeeeathhhh!*" she cried.

Again I was reminded of Charles Laughton begging for water in the village square. In the distance, I heard sirens that mingled eerily with the sound of Alice's wailing.

The black kid's chest suddenly hitched in a gasp. He sat up, rubbed the back of his head, and looked at the blood on his hand. His friend became manic, laughing and gibbering. Then went suddenly quiet as Alice's shadow fell on him.

She rose inch by inch, began trudging past her two tormentors, who watched her without comment. She wiped tears from her misshapen face as she hobbled to the bus stop and collapsed on the bench. The guy from the Beamer walked on rubber legs to the sidewalk, where he sat on the curb and looked around with glassy eyes. The black guy got to his feet and wiped his hand on his jeans. He looked fine. He and his buddy approached Alice tentatively, then sat on either side of her and spoke to her gently while they all waited together for the cops to show up.

As I watched I saw a pair of punk rock girls parade by on the sidewalk. They glanced at Alice, then turned their faces quickly away from her, in my direction.

They were laughing.

ABOUT THE AUTHOR

Israel Finn is a horror, dark fantasy, and speculative fiction writer. He's had a life-long love affair with books, and was weaned on authors like Kurt Vonnegut, Ray Bradbury, Richard Matheson, Edgar Rice Burroughs, and H.G. Wells. Books were always strewn everywhere about the big white house in the Midwest where he grew up.

He loves literary works, but his main fascination lies in the fantastic and the macabre.

Later he discovered Robert McCammon, Dean Koontz, F. Paul Wilson, Dan Simmons, Ramsey Campbell, and Stephen King, as well as several others, and the die was indelibly cast.

He's been a factory worker, a delivery driver, a singer/songwriter in several rock bands, and a sailor, among other things. But throughout he's always maintained his love of storytelling.

israelfinn.com